GODS, DREAMS & LOVE

BY GERALD G. GRIFFIN

TITLE: Gods, Dreams & Love

ISBN: 978-1-7345724-4-5 (e-book)
ISBN: 978-1-7345724-5-2 (paperback)

Library of Congress Catalog Card Number: 2020909186

1st Edition

ALSO BY GERALD G. GRIFFIN

The Gods of Winter
Of Good & Evil
The Corruptors
The Last Coming
The Death Disciple

For Jane A. Valentine

CHAPTER 1

IT'S ALWAYS SOMETHING. This something began when Frank Worsly, leader of the wealthy and secret society, the Fraternity, arrived at my lake house in a new Mercedes.

"Don't worry, Gloria, I'll get rid of him." I said, looking out the window, as Frank approached the front of the house. Making his way through the unlocked front door, Frank stepped inside.

"I wasn't expecting company," I said, struggling to find some sense of hospitality, and making a mental note that I need to learn to lock the damned door.

Frank, as usual, wore a tailored suit, this one dark blue-pinstriped, which lent his six-foot stature the look of a refined executive. I hadn't shaved in weeks, and the last time I wore a suit my life was a hell of a lot better. I noticed dark lines and shadows beneath Frank's striking green eyes. He was preoccupied about something. The something that brought him here unannounced and would make it difficult to send him on his way.

"It's been a while, Bob, how have you been?" he said, with a thin, reluctant smile on his face.

"You stopped by to ask me that?"

"No. Am I interrupting something?"

"I'm having a tough time pulling myself together since Gloria's death," I said.

"That's why we've left you alone."

"Okay, then why the visit?"

"You and I need to talk, Bob."

"Talk about what?"

"We need your help."

"For God's sake, I'm in no condition to help anyone!"

"Bob, you're the only one who can save the Fraternity."

"Me, the only one? What are you bullshitting me about?"

"There's an elite and powerful group, the Cyprus Group–survivors of the deeps state's swamp, bastards with no regard for the sanctity of life, bent on wiping us out... murdering each one of us."

"Murder?! Hell, Frank, this is something for the police, and other law enforcement authorities to handle."

"The authorities won't touch them! They have access to crucial strategies pursued by our government and control over US gold reserves. The Cyprus Group deploys hit men, depending on location and situation. On the US Mexico Border, under the direction of the Mexican Cartel, Al Queda Arabs and sometimes American assassins are assigned to targets. It's near impossible to link any crimes committed to their organization, and their reach extends to Europe, the far East, even China."

"So, what are you saying Frank?"

"I'm saying, they will stop at nothing to end our existence–right down to the last member, including you!"

"How am I supposed to help? And you better damn well come up with something other than I'm the only one who can save us!"

"Got a drink?"

"No damn drink, Frank. Enough time wasted. Just get the hell on with it!"

"All right, all right, but give me a calm ear."

Frank paused, taking on a strained composure. Then, with measured words, he set forth a murderous scheme, one leaving me aghast.

"My God, Frank, you, of all people, are asking me to track down and kill?! Murder these schemers whom you regard as our enemy? Well, forget it. I'm no killer! What you propose is at odds with everything the Fraternity stands for."

"There is no other way! We must do the unthinkable. Bob, no matter how much you don't like it, we have to do something about this, or we'll all die!" Frank's eyes were penetrating, and his voice returned to the quiet eloquence of strength and authority as he made his case.

"Don't you understand? This is our only option. I'm not asking you to kill–just organize it."

"I want no part in this! I have my sanity back, and you can bet your sweet ass I'm keeping it."

"I see. Would you prefer then the insanity the

Cyprus Group will inflict upon us if left unopposed to pursue its rampage and murder all members of the Fraternity, including your sweet ass and mine? Are you saying that you, a trusted member, will throw away their lives without lifting a hand to stop it? Will that help you hang on to your sanity?" He stepped closer and placed his hand on my right shoulder as if appealing to my sense of duty and honor.

"Christ, Bob, we are counting on you for our lives!"

"Are you implying the members have agreed to this? Are in on this killing spree?"

"Yes. All of them."

"There must be another way without murder."

Frank began pacing the room and pondering aloud. "How do you handle a crazed grizzly charging at you? You either shoot it, right on the spot, or it damn well finishes you in gruesome agony." Then stopping to look at me, he said, "Bob, this is what we're facing. We don't have the luxury of debating our action during the charge."

"Frank, I'm in no condition to cope with what you're asking me to do. Please leave me out of it! Have you no mercy?"

"The question is," he said, "do you have the heart to save your colleagues, all of whom are loyal to you, none of whom would ever let you down?"

"But damn it, Frank! This is not a question of heart! You're crazier than I ever was if you think I can perform some kind of magic that will save everyone. I can't even save myself."

"You're wrong, Bob!"

"Wrong? Have you gone mad?"

"Bob, it was your madness that helped me figure out the key to saving our members."

"What do you mean, my madness?"

"God only knows what restored your mind, but after they confined you to the sanitarium, while you were deemed insane, you displayed it! Bob, your insanity revealed the solution I was looking for. You have the crucial killer instinct that no other member, me included, possesses. Your killer instinct, that is our saving grace!"

Now I was certain Frank was mad. I said, "I hate to be rude and inhospitable to a dear friend, but Frank, do me a favor, get the hell out of my house and leave me alone!"

"This is dereliction of duty, unforgivable!"

"You best get going or there's no telling what my killer instinct will do to you."

"I'm leaving," but heed my warning, and watch your step."

CHAPTER 2

WHEN FRANK LEFT, his fear for the Fraternity's fate left with him, for I immediately dispelled it as a possible symptom of paranoia. I had been declared sane, but I had my doubts. As for Frank, I wasn't sure which of the two of us was the crazier? I turned my attention back to the conversation I was attempting to have before Frank showed up.

"Sorry I took so long. That Frank is something else." I listened for a response. As always, there was only silence. The hidden edge of my continuing insanity, I didn't want to admit, was Gloria. She was dead and all I could think about was stalking her spirit. I felt a compulsion to see and speak to it, as if her spirit could be summoned from the impenetrable mist of the beyond. I was haunted by my memories. Especially the final ones before she left me for good.

"The pain!" Gloria's voice contorted by agony as she gasped for air replayed in my mind. I could still remember how helpless I felt as her hand clutched at the left side of her torso and she cried out to me.

"Oh, Bob... Bob! The pain is terrible! What is happening to me?" She couldn't have known she was facing the mystical force of the Gods of Winter. They were trying to get at me, and they were the cause of the mysterious and escalating deterioration of her health.

I didn't have time to say goodbye before she died. But worse, I felt responsible for her death. I should have protected her from the Gods. Will she ever forgive me? That was my haunting. A haunting that tore away pieces of my soul whenever I recalled last seeing her alive. She was suffering from severe brain damage in a deep coma and on life support. Her body hooked up to a monitor, an IV, and a ventilator and jerking in involuntary spasms. Her doctor's words echoing in my mind.

"With the severity of her brain damage, she will never come out of her coma... never recover. She is not with us. Never will be with us."

On my next visit to the hospital she was dead. The sight of her body, her face, once so alive and sparkling with life, was devoid of her loving spirit. She was no more. Unable to bear the shock of my overwhelming loss, I was placed in a sanitarium. The head psychiatrist concluded that I was a hopeless case.

"Doctor Daniels' mental faculties have been shattered. The intensity of his deteriorated mental state renders him beyond any form of treatment. And this is the state in which he is expected to remain until he dies." Against all odds, I escaped the clutches of madness and recovered completely. I was diagnosed as cured and sane and was released back into society. I returned to the lake house. But ever since then the

Fraternity had lost all meaning for me, though officially I was still a member. Frank had been a close and reliable friend once so I put up with his visit as long as I could. For old time's sake. But that was another time.

My time now is for Gloria who left her mark on my heart; whose untimely death has reduced my existence to wallowing in memories of all that she was. The wonder of her being. The enchantment of her graceful comportment. The freshness of her vibrant beauty. The soft melody of her voice. The joy of her love and spirit, where just the sparkle of her eyes awakened every cell in my body to the gift of her happiness. My time is hers now. The memory of her everywhere in the lake house. What she said there. What she read. What she wrote. What made her laugh. What made her cry. And adorning the walls, her paintings, created from the strokes of her brush rendering each work a song from the soul of all her creations.

Gloria's rare lust for life surrounded me even in her eternal absence. Even though I am sane again, I can't accept that Gloria is gone! Lost to the shadows of time, as I am left to face the painful reality that I have lost her. Forever. I am overwhelmed by the constant craving to see her, speak with her, and hear her whisper to me once more.

"I love you." Deep down I suspect my yearning to make contact with her spirit was borne from something more, the selfish need to ask her for forgiveness. Her spirit is out there somewhere. It has to be!

"Gloria, is your spirit with me? Can you hear me?

I miss you so. Can you speak to me?" Nothing but silence.

"What am I doing?" I said aloud. This is insane. I am compelled to connect with her spirit, even if I don't know how.

"I try again on several occasions talking into an empty room, and each time the same result, silence!

"Damn!" What if being dead means just that? You're dead! Shut out from any afterlife existence. No spirit lingering about like in the movies and stories about unsettled souls. I just couldn't accept that. I changed my tactics. Stopped asking for her to appear and speak to me and instead began having conversations. I left it up to her spirit to decide if it wanted to join me or not.

"Gloria, I love you. I miss you. I wish you were here. You having a nice time in eternity? They better be taking care of my princess. I hope it is a place deserving of you." I put on some soft music.

"Gloria, you will love this music... the kind you liked to dance to. Ah, how I miss your warm gentle touch when we danced. How about a dance, Gloria? Nothing fancy, just the Two-step. Do they allow spirits to dance?" I got no dance.

"What am I doing wrong?" Then an unexpected revelation stuck me. It's the setting. Gloria's spirit will only appear and speak to me at the place she loves the most, her favorite place.

"That has to be it!" I ran out the front door and down the sloping green lawn and bore left just past a small firing range I used for shooting my pistol and keeping my eyes sharp. I was headed for a grassy path that led to a short pier. On each side the ground curved out from the shore to form a cozy cove, and beyond was a breathtaking view of Lake Lanier. This cove was Gloria's favorite place.

The first time we made the excursion from the lake house we were holding hands, laughing, running free, the breeze ruffling through her hair, and a bright gleam of joy striking across her eyes. We were like children chasing rainbows, oblivious to the cares of the world. I slowed down and strolled down to the end of the pier. The sun was now on its western slant. I decided not to push right away for the appearance of her spirit, but to allow the cove's peaceful allure to soak into my psyche. An occasional largemouth bass leapt out of the water, twisting and turning in grand fashion before splashing back beneath the surface. I allowed myself the luxury of reveling in the memory of the last time Gloria was with me on this pier. I had watched her gaze out over the water.

"Oh, it's... it's so beautiful, darling! I love it here! Our own private bay. This is my favorite place." She said before one of her irrepressible expressions of joy overtook her and she kicked off her shoes, and in willowy grace bounded off the pier and onto the sandy beach. I took in every movement of her body, pirouetting across the sand to the sounds of her own laughter. She knew how to enjoy the gifts of nature, and now in her absence, with tears stinging my eyes, I realize that she too was a gift of nature. A gift of glorious radiance, near infinite vitality, and an unending zest for life.

Then my eyes were drawn upward to where the beach sloped up to meet the forest's edge. Standing there, motionless, looking in my direction, was a magnificent buck with a majestic rack of antlers. I had seen it before, when Gloria spoke softly to it. It was one of Gloria's forest friends. Our eyes locked before it gently hoofed the ground, and emitted a melancholic bellow, and I could swear I saw a tear in its eye. In that moment, I was certain that even creatures of the forest suffered from Gloria's absence. Even the trees seemed to emit a rustling wail of sorrowful murmurs in the breeze. I felt this was my moment and finally spoke.

"These are your friends, Gloria. Their hearts ache too because you're gone. Let your spirit appear before us. Speak to us. Speak to me." I waited… and waited, and listened, and watched, and waited. Nothing! Worse than nothing, not even a hint of her spiritual presence… or message. I stood still and silent, my eyes burning as I watched the sun making its final descent. Its soft orange glow sinking into the horizon as if bidding me one final, sad, farewell. My hopes died with that sun. But I just had to see her. Needed to speak with her.

This notwithstanding, and with a sadness beyond description, I mumbled, "Gloria, I'll never see or speak to your spirit."

CHAPTER 3

FOLLOWING MY DISHEARTENING VISIT to the cove, the gray-blue edge of dusk was frosting with stars upon my approach to the lake house. I felt worn out and emotionally drained. I sometimes referred to the lake house as the "bungalow". It was my retreat from the rest of the world.

The house was on a small hill in a large clearing and surrounded by nature. The only entrance which I kept closed was through a private gate. Out front and to the left, a vast emerald lawn sloped downward toward a rustic road. To the right a narrower lawn, bright green, also sloping downward. The forest's rich foliage beginning at its furthest edge and close to my pistol firing range. The end of the road below abruptly curved upward and in between the two lawns, was the drive. I pulled open the screened porch door and then another which led into the largest room in the house, the living room, and flipped on a light.

A grand marble fireplace with a brass screen in front of it highlighted the back wall. Save for some lavish touches I had added from time to time, the furnishings of this room, the kitchen, the small guest bedroom, the main bedroom and the bathroom were fairly basic, but sturdy, and suited for a lake house retreat. I intended to make my way into the compact kitchen to search for leftovers in the fridge when a sudden drowsiness swept over me and I couldn't fight it off. I didn't make it past the living room sofa and felt my body collapse and fall into an immediate slumber. I was dreaming, but unlike ordinary dreams where everything becomes fragmented and lacking in coherence, my dreaming was in a place that seemed as solid as the real world.

My senses heightened, I stood still as I felt a gentle breeze caress my face and took in the cloudless afternoon sky burned by the sun's everchanging palette of red and orange. The sunbaked golden landscape, the rolling desert vista, and the sand and rocks beneath my feet that seemed to have no end mesmerized me. In the distance, the peaks of mountains dotted the horizon. I felt calm, at peace, and a hint of excitement brewing as I thought back to the breeze in the cove saying, "In a dream." This was it. The dream in which the breeze said I would see Gloria's spirit.

"This is a heavenly welcome, Gloria," I said with a growing feeling of elation.

"Where are you?" I saw no one. Then, a misty figure that seemed to float across the sand was moving toward me. "Gloria?"

The desert was changing before my eyes. Countless hummingbirds hovered below a brilliant sun-kissed sky and above the vibrant green blooms of summer. Juniper trees, sagebrush, even the scrubbrush alive with color. The air sweet and invigorating. When the figure was almost upon me, my heart sank. It wasn't Gloria. Who is this intruder? A tall man with a golden tan, squared off features, dark keen eyes, wearing a white shirt and faded blue denims approached. It was hard to tell how old he was, but his glowing skin made it appear he was brimming with health.

"Hi, Doctor Daniels," he said. His voice deep and serene.

"Or do you prefer I call you Bob?"

"Where's Gloria? I want to see Gloria. Where is she? You're not supposed to be here, who the hell are you?"

"You may call me Cyd," the man smiled, a certain twinkle in his eyes.

"You might say I am a celestial helper."

"Then help me find Gloria… her spirit. I need to speak with it. That's why I'm here."

"All will make sense soon enough," Cyd smiled. He placed his soft hand on my own and led me forward.

"Come, there is someone waiting to speak with you."

"Who?"

"You will see." Before, I could object, we were floating across the desert toward Pinion trees in the distant foothills where magnificent mountains reflecting the sun's vivid, dazzling hues lay in wait. The view was so breathtaking it rendered me speechless. We reached an oasis, a pool of deep, clear blue water surrounded by a lush carpet of the greenest grass, the reddest wildflowers and still more Juniper and Pinon trees.

By the edge of the pool, an older man with a weathered, ageless face waited. His sandy, wavy hair lifting easily in the gentle breeze as he cooked what appeared to be small meatballs over a fire. His unimposing frame dressed in khaki pants, a short-sleeved shirt and sandals, he looked anything but omnipotent, but I got the sense he was.

"I will leave you now," Cyd said, smiling. Then he vanished. The older man looked up from his cooking, and said, "Ah, yes, Bob." His voice was soothing and laced with easy charm, and when he looked at me, the blue of his eyes made me think of the ocean.

"Sit down beside me," he said, motioning with his hand to an empty space by the edge of the pool. Whoever this man was, he was likeable, which helped ease my misgivings about the dream so far.

"I don't know what this cookout is all about, I'm here for only one reason. To see and speak to Gloria's spirit."

"Yes, quite a trying time you are having with that futile venture."

"How do you know that?"

"In a dream, does it matter?" the man smiled. There was an amusing, infectious glint in his eyes that created an internal struggle to stay on task. I wanted to speak to Gloria's spirit.

"If you want this dream to continue, you better tell me who you are, then bring forth Gloria's spirit pronto. Otherwise, I'm out of here!"

"You may call me Pleasant. As to bringing forth Gloria's spirit, that is not within my providence–not without permission."

"Permission from whom?"

"Why an old friend of yours," Pleasant replied, unable to suppress his obvious amusement.

"The one who lifted you permanently out of your state of madness."

"God?!"

"We lesser providences refer to Him as Nice. God is an earthly indulgence. Here, the term god is how we refer to those in these lesser providences, all of whom are under the ruling Providence of Nice's watchful eye,"

What a weird dream, I thought. "So you are one of these lesser gods?"

"Yes."

I couldn't resist asking, "And what is your providence? What do you do?"

Pleasant laughed. "Whatever Nice calls upon me to do." His laugh easing into a grin, he said, "One thing I do, you already know. For humans who qualify, with the aid of one of my helpers, such as Cyd, I drive them into madness. We are the Gods of Winter." I felt a surge of adrenaline.

"The Gods of Winter? You, unholy bastard! You, you killed Gloria! Wracked her body with pain, caused her to suffer and die to get to me and drive me mad."

"Nice got on me about that," Pleasant grinned. I

had to stop myself from attacking him. This is only a dream. A silly dream. The Gods of Winter dragged out of my psyche, so they could taunt me. I played along. Had to play along and keep my focus on why I was having this dream, Gloria's spirit. Could I get him to make her spirit appear? That's what I needed to focus on.

"No hard feelings?" Pleasant asked, still grinning.

"None," I said.

"Splendid!" Pleasant nodded. With a hint of cheer in his voice, he once again motioned for me to join him.

"Sit down beside me." I sat and watched as he used odd looking prongs to place what looked like meatballs onto a small plate that had just appeared. He held a plate in front of me, his smile never faltering.

"Here, have some. They will do wonders for you." He then served himself and with his fingers lifted a meatball to his mouth and chewed on it with gusto. I used my fingers to pop one into my mouth and felt pleasantly surprised at how delicious it was. I eagerly ate another. We sat there, the only sound our grunts of satisfaction as we savored each lip-smacking bite. My mood had lifted. Placing my empty plate on the grass, Pleasant beamed, "You feel better?"

"Damn right! I feel terrific! Now all I need is to speak with Gloria's spirit."

"Nice will not allow that."

"Why not?"

"Nice has something in mind for you. Something you must handle through me and my providence." Still, feeling euphoric from the effect of the meatballs, I managed a smile, and said, "The hell with that, that just makes no sense."

"Bob, a mortal cannot comprehend the goings on here. You cannot possibly understand the what or why of what we do. But if you wish to see and speak to Gloria's spirit, I suggest you listen to what I have to say."

"Okay. I'll listen. But it better lead to letting me see and speak to Gloria's spirit."

"Hold that thought," he said, still smiling.

"What is this all about?"

"The folly of your world. In particular, the folly which you and your friend, Frank Worsly, and your Fraternity friends, are the object of. Bad folly." Upon hearing those words, the calm euphoria I had a moment ago seemed to slip away. This guy's really digging into my mind.

"Bad folly?"

"Yes. A folly of ruthlessness we know will lead others to commit heinous atrocities against innocents. All for the sake of power." I couldn't help thinking those thoughts are definitely not in my psyche.

"I must stop these transgressors and I need your help. Frank made you an offer, accept it, organize a plan and see it through."

"Wait, Nice would okay this?"

"Yes."

"I don't believe it! How could Nice approve something this ungodly?"

"You are not a student of history, are you? As I have told you, the logic and morality of what we do here is way beyond a human mortal's comprehension."

"They may be beyond my comprehension, but one thing I do understand is that I want nothing to do with these killings!"

"Now... now, don't react so impulsively," Pleasant said. That did it! I'd had it with this dream.

"I'm fed up with your damn smiling, and this damn dream. So, buddy, do me a favor and smile me the hell out of it!" Immediately, I awoke, my skin covered in sweat.

CHAPTER 4

I AWAKENED FROM THE DREAM feeling like I had a tenuous hold on reality. My body was trembling and my mind foggy. My smartphone chirped into the room's silence, giving me no time to dwell on my discomfort. Frank's name popped up on the caller ID, so I hesitated before answering.

"Frank."

"Bob, it's happening! Faster than we could have expected. Those bastards killed Chris Moynihan... took out his guard too. And they shot Ben Winters. He's in the hospital in critical condition!"

"My God!" Chris and Ben had been two of my closest Fraternity friends. Part of me refused to accept this, I wasn't sure how to react.

"What's Ben's prognosis?" was all I could manage.

"Not good, Bob. He's in bad shape, but able to speak now and then. He wants to see you... as do I. There's a jet with security guards on its way to you, Dave's on it along with security escorts. They'll pick you up at your local airport and bring you back here. Do you have your pistol?"

"Not anymore."

"Shit!" Frank almost never cursed.

"Keep your guard up on your drive to the airport,

and until Dave gets you safely on the plane, you must be cautious of strangers approaching you." Dave Rommairone was tall and lean and a psychiatrist when he was accepted into the Fraternity. He was now engaged to another Fraternity member, Kym Pedalecki, both of them friends I cherished for having come to my aid while I was in the sanitarium. When we arrived at the Michigan Medical School hospital, Dave and I accompanied by three brawny guards, took a private elevator up to Ben's room in the Critical Care Unit.

By the looks of it, aside from a hiring frenzy of armed guards, Frank had also used his influence as former Dean of the medical school, and leader of the Fraternity to ensure Ben got the care he needed under the highest security protocols possible. The potent hospital smell assaulted my senses and brought on an involuntary shudder. Dave and I entered Ben's room and found another guard stationed at the window, a nurse taking Ben's vitals, and Frank by his bedside. Dave stayed back near the closed door, while I slowly made my way toward the hospital bed. Frank looked relieved to see me, but there was a glum expression on his face, and he looked haggard, and washed over by emotional fatigue.

I reached Frank's side and looked down at the pitiful sight that was now Ben Winters. Ben had sponsored me into the Fraternity and like Frank, Dave and Kym had refused to give up on me and expected I'd make a full recovery. Ben's body lay motionless in his thin gray hospital gown. The monitors and beeping consoles hooked up to his body brought back another wave of unpleasant memories. There were splints on both his legs, bandages covering a torso riddled by purple splotches that formed his bullet wounds.

I wanted to look into his face, find a hint of his energetic disposition, but the bandages with slits for his eyes, nose and mouth made that impossible.

"He's lucky he's still breathing," Frank said. I reached down and gently squeezed Ben's hand. I wanted him to know I was there for him, but when his eyes filled with pain, opened and locked with mine, Ben whispered through a voice scratched raw from his ordeal. In a barely audible whisper, he said, "Bob... Bob, get 'em, get 'em." His voice almost faltered as he added, "But watch it... watch it. They're tricky, so tricky."

The nurse in attendance quietly interjected, "Mr. Worsly, it's best he keeps quiet. I would suggest you let him get some rest, both of you should get some rest." Frank stepped away from Ben's hospital bed, he was clearly on edge and in need of sleep, but he motioned for me and Dave to follow. We huddled together away from Ben's bed and I caught Frank looking over his shoulder out the window several times before he finally spoke.

"They could strike any of us, at any time," Frank warned.

"We must remain suspicious of anyone we don't know. Protect ourselves at all times, not only with guards, but keeping ourselves armed." He looked like a man shouldering a heavy burden.

"If only they'd been carrying a gun."

"But hell, Frank," Dave, visibly shaken, interjected, "None of us, except for Bob, who's a good shot with a pistol knows how to use a gun."

"Then the rest of us better damn well learn, and fast!"

"Do the police know who murdered Chris?" I asked.

Frank let out an exasperated sigh. "No. They're clueless. Same with Ben. I suspect the Cyprus Group is using hit men. I already told you how they operate Bob. They're scattered across the country and well concealed from the public eye." Wanting no part of this discussion, I changed the subject.

"When is Chris's funeral?"

"There won't be a funeral, we can't risk it. I persuaded his wife to cremate his body. If we survive what we're facing, we can hold a memorial service for Chris at a later date. Let's just hope his will be the only one. Bob, I hate to have to say this again, you can prevent these memorials. If you organize the plan to kill off the Cyprus Group, we'll be free of this threat once and for all. For God's sake, for Chris and Ben's sake, for the others, you must do what I'm asking, begging you to do!"

I wish Frank could understand that other than

extending these warranted courtesies to our friends, I can't do what he asked. Connecting with Gloria's spirit is all I want to do now.

"Frank, I can't track down the members of the Cyprus Group any more than anyone else in the Fraternity. I've told you I want no part in these killings and that's final!" Frank looked away from me, "Then God help us!"

"I'll protect myself, and I won't ask that anyone else put their life in jeopardy to do so. Look Frank, I'll keep tabs on Ben, but I need to go home now." Frank looked at Dave, "Take Bob home. But get some rest, both of you. I'll arrange for a safe room in the hospital, where you can sleep." The following morning, Dave and I, joined by three guards, boarded a 45M Learjet. The Fraternity owned a fleet of ten. The jet's interior resembled a first-class lounge and could comfortably seat six. All around the cabin, wood trimming, leather seating and even a sofa, all the makings of luxury travel. Our flight was in the skillful hands of a Fraternity hired pilot, who like all the others was discreet and loyal. Two of the guards stationed themselves on the sofa, their eyes already alert and trained on the aircraft's windows. Dave and the other guard took the two front row seats, and I sat in one of the two seats directly behind them. I'd told Dave before boarding I wanted to sit alone during the flight.

I needed some time to collect my thoughts and the flight to Georgia gave me the perfect opportunity to do just that. The engines roared and thundered down the runway before lifting and climbing into a near cloudless sky. The weather was clear, which meant the odds of turbulence were low.

About fifty minutes after takeoff, I felt that overwhelming drowsy feeling overtake me. I could not resist falling asleep, and felt my head fall back against the seat cushion. Cyd did not greet me this time, and I found myself once again by the oasis where Pleasant was sitting on the grass and peering out over the pool's deep blue water.

"Why have you dragged me back into this silly dream?" Pleasant turned to look at me.

"As you know Bob, our last conversation, was, should we say, interrupted?"

"Look I don't care to continue that conversation with you." Pleasant rose to his feet.

"Not even for a warning?"

"Warning? A warning about what?"

"I can see you are too tense Bob, perhaps a drink will help you relax?" He looked at me with that incessant smile again.

"You really need to relax." Before I could reply, a small goblet containing what looked like bubbling champagne popped up in my hand.

"Oh, no! I'm not touching this stuff. You're not tricking me into anything."

"A pity," Pleasant said, his smile unwavering. I'd had it with his damned smiling and luring me into dreams against my will. I hurled the goblet and its contents onto the grass, then said, "The only thing that will keep me hanging around in this dream is if you bring forth Gloria's spirit!"

"You know the conditions for that."

"I told you, I'm not killing anyone! I am not a killer!"

"But you do have a firing range. Only lawmen, the military and killers have these. And you are not part of the first two."

"That was only to prepare me for self-defense. Look, I'm sick of you and this stupid dream. Get me the hell out of here!"

"Without hearing my warning?"

"Forget it! I'm sick of warnings too. I've had enough of them. Just leave me alone. Got that?!" The next thing I knew Dave was shaking me on the shoulder.

"Bob, Bob, wake up!"

"What?" I muttered, disoriented, blinking my eyes.

"Where are we?"

"On approach to the Lee Gilmer Memorial Airport in Gainesville."

The jet halted on the tarmac just a short distance away from the central airport gates. As it was being refueled, two of the guards, their weapons at the ready had their eye on anyone approaching the aircraft, including those tasked with refueling. Dave had given them their orders.

"If you see anything suspicious, shoot first, ask questions later." The third guard remained on the aircraft with Dave and me. Before deplaning, I said to

Dave, "Thanks for the ride. And congratulations on your engagement to Kym, she's terrific! Better take care of her, protect her." Dave rubbed his chin uneasily.

"Thanks. But that seems like an insurmountable task given the situation we're in. Kym hates guns. She hates carrying one and doesn't know what to do with one, anyway." With a pleading look in his gentle, blue eyes, he looked at me and grabbed hold of my left arm just as I was about to leave.

"Bob, the best protection for Kym is if you accept what Frank has asked of you. You have a knack for survival. The rest of us don't. I pray you reconsider Frank's request." I took a moment before responding.

"Sorry, Dave, I just can't do that. Goodbye." With that, and with the guards outside giving the okay, I deplaned the jet and accompanied by one guard walked across the grassy verge toward where I'd parked. Once I was alone again a nagging question formed itself in my mind. What warning had Pleasant intended to give me?

CHAPTER 5

I FELT ON EDGE and like my life was becoming an episode of the Twilight Zone. On the drive from the airport to the lake house, as I promised Dave, I didn't let down my guard once. As I expected, during the drive in my eight-year-old Cadillac Deville, which was still riding nicely, I met with no undue incident.

Once inside the house, I found everything there to be normal. The only thing keeping me from feeling relaxed now was my need to urinate. It had been a hectic morning. Just as I was about to relieve myself, I realized the toilet had somehow clogged up. I turned on the faucets, there was no running water. Damn!

Living in a remote location meant I still had to resort to the Yellow Pages when I needed services. I came to the section listing plumbers and went down the list, phoning each one, and received the same response:

"Sorry, we can't get anyone out to you today. Would you like to schedule for tomorrow? We will try our best to fit you in." Having no bottled water, and not keen on using the outdoors as an out-house, I said to each person I spoke to:

"If you find a plumber, please get in touch." I left my

name, phone number, and address. I was about ready to give up on receiving a call when a white van, BUSBY PLUMBING neatly imprinted on its side in blue letters, pulled into the drive, and parked behind my Cadillac. A rugged man, a little over six feet, dressed in a light brown workman's garb, exited the van. As he approached, I noticed he was carrying a workman's kit, and around his waist he wore a wide belt crammed with an assortment of tools and gadgets, including what looked like a sheathed knife. I held the open front door as he made his way toward me.

"Am I ever glad to see you? I'm really grateful you could make it out here today."

"I understand you need a plumber," the man said, amiably returning my smile. His voice was softer than I expected. His hair was black, neatly combed above a well-proportioned face, eyes darkly brown, making me think of black velvet.

"Had a cancelation, and could fit you in, name's Carl Busby." His smile eased into a consoling expression, "Now, what's your plumbing problem?"

"No running water, follow me and I'll show you." I had taken only a few steps when I felt the hard blow of a blunt object hit the back of my skull. I let out a moan in response to the pain and could not break my fall; I was dizzy and on the verge of blacking out. Somehow, a surge of adrenalin enabled me to remain conscious, but I would not let Carl know that, not yet. I realized I had invited my executioner in and I had to think fast if I had any hope of surviving.

I laid still in the prone position, feigning unconsciousness, while quietly attempting to resurrect whatever strength I could muster. Carl was still somewhere behind me. I heard him set down his work kit and open it. I had to act and hope the adrenalin coursing through my body was enough to get me out of this. With the same innate speed and agility from my high school football days, I forcefully rolled my body into Carl's legs and threw him off-balance, which dislodged a 9mm pistol with a silencer from his hand and I watched it land on the floor and out of his immediate reach before I shot back up onto my feet.

For a moment, there was silence as we both just stood there staring at one another, my vision still blurry. Then Carl, with the mocking smile of a brutal killer on his face, quipped disdainfully, "I don't need a weapon to kill you!" Then he lunged at me with the hardness of lethal intent and grabbed my body and slammed it to the floor. Carl had the greater advantage, his strength and my inability to shake off the dizziness. I could tell he'd intended for my death to be quick. He bashed me on the side of the head with his fist and used his enormous hands to grip me tightly by the throat. With his thumbs on my windpipe, he choked me, and my mouth popping open, my dazed eyes darted about as pain nearly overcame my body.

I fought off the agony of my inevitable end and clutched desperately at the sides of his torso. Then my right hand felt it. The sheathed double blade knife on his belt. With what energy I had left, my breath thickening, I grabbed the knife's handle, pulled it out of its sheath, and with the force of a bent bow suddenly released I rammed the sharp steel into Carl's rib cage.

"AAHHHGG!!!" Carl screamed and let go of his grip on me. His body jerked upwards and backwards in his attempt to get erect on his feet. I saw the blood seep through his shirt and ooze down his trousers from where the knife blade had penetrated his flesh. I remembered the 9mm and although still disoriented and struggling to breathe normally, I dragged my body across the floor to where I knew it had fallen. I grabbed it, raised my back up off the floor just enough to release the safety catch, point the muzzle and squeeze the trigger.

The bullet sliced through the side of Carl's neck and severed his artery, which caused more blood to spew. Carl helplessly clutched at his windpipe, his throat squeezed shut and his legs quivered before his body finally toppled to the floor. I lowered my arm, dropped the pistol, and rested the back of my head on the floor. Emotionally spent, and physically exhausted, I just laid there, shivering, sucking in deep breaths.

My head was throbbing, everything spinning around me, I could barely think, I felt like a boxer who had taken the ten count. I knew I had better make a call and let Frank know about my war trophy. When I finally got him on the phone, my mind was so jumpy I struggled to remain coherent.

"Dave is on the way," Frank said.

"Stay put! Do nothing. Don't speak to anyone. And stay clear of the body." Once I got off the phone, I hobbled into the bathroom, and peered into the mirror with the intention of patching myself up. The reflection I saw unsettled me. In less than two hours after phoning Frank, Dave and two guards showed up in a rented car.

"Jesus!" Dave said, a look of disbelief on his face as he surveyed the bloody mess in the living room and the dead body on the floor.

"You're lucky to be alive! Frank would have come here himself, but shortly before you called, they found Meredith Chambers murdered. Frank wants us to get rid of the evidence, the last thing we need is the cops snooping around."

"Oh, Christ!" I said. Meredith and Gloria had been close.

"The murders are happening faster now." Dave said, almost to himself.

"Dave, is Ben still alive?"

"Yeah. He's holding on. Your visit helped. The doctors now think he has a slight chance of recovering." I sighed with relief, but as I looked into Dave's face all I saw was fear.

"Bob, right now we are all concerned about you. You were fortunate enough to stave off this hit man, but next time you won't be so lucky. Frank doesn't want to lose you, so I will leave one of these guards with you. One of the best of the lot for your protection." I nodded at the 9mm pistol lying on the floor.

"I'm armed now, I don't need an armed guard too."

"Frank insists! You are the one member the Fraternity cannot afford to lose."

"I think you and Frank have overestimated my value."

"With this blatant attempt on your life, surely you will take heed and reconsider Frank's request."

"Dave, what Frank wants is downright illogical. What he expects is impossible. Dave, it's an absurd notion, pure fantasy!" He looked at me for a long moment, his blue eyes desperate.

"Bob, we're running out of options, all Frank is asking is that you try! Just think about it while we clean up this bloody mess, I can't stay too long."

The man calling himself Carl had no identification on his body. We found no identification in the van either, where the two guards Dave brought with him dumped his blanket-wrapped corpse. The guards were busy inspecting the outside of the property and quickly found the plumbing pipes Carl tinkered with.

Inside the house, using a bleach and water solution Dave brought with him, we got to work on cleaning up the splotches of blood and getting rid of any evidence. When it was time to leave, one guard drove off in the plumbing van. And Dave got into the rented car, but before driving off we exchanged a few more words.

"We will dispose of the corpse and the van. I will see to it you get a real plumber out here." Then he handed me a cell phone.

"From now on, use this cell for all your calls. It's cloned. Untraceable. And stay off the computer. And Bob, what do I tell Frank as to your intentions?"

"Tell him I'm trying to clear my mind."

"That's it?"

"That's it," I said.

"You had better clear your mind quickly! Time's running out."

"Dave, thank you for all you've done for me today." I placed my hand on his shoulder.

"I owe you. Give my regards to Kym."

"I will, Bob. She's climbing the walls! These aren't exactly the happiest of days."

"Those days are behind us."

"Yeah, I've got to go." Bernie Coyle was the guard Dave insisted stay behind for my protection. Regarded as one of the best from the guard pool, Bernie was broad-shouldered, muscular, tough-minded and seasoned. He had a beak-nosed face and a vigilant eye, now devoted to me, his services paid for by Frank out of a special Fraternity fund. Bernie also had an arsenal of weapons, pistols, grenades, knives, even a machete, and a submachine gun. Heaven help any innocent person wandering onto the property by accident.

"You as good as they say you are?" I asked Bernie. With one of his rare grins, his voice a gravely, heavy rasp, he answered, "No hit man'll ever get in here... or even close, and still be breathin'." I believed him.

Bernie knew a plumber, sent by Dave, would

arrive shortly and so as not to scare him off, I confined Bernie to the guest bedroom where he could keep the door closed but remain vigilant and at the ready should something go wrong. When Al, an older man on the thinner side, arrived to fix the plumbing, I first directed him to the outside of the house. When he finished his work there, and entered the house to do his inside work, he gave me a strange look and said, "Someone did a fancy job screwing up your pipes out there."

"Halloween came early, I said. Appreciate you putting everything in back in order."

Once the plumbing was running back to normal, I wrote Al a check for his services. No sooner had he left, than Bernie shot out of the guest bedroom like an unleashed Siberian tiger.

"Everything okay, boss?" he rasped, darting about from room to room.

"The water's running. The toilet works, and the plumber didn't even try to kill me."

"No more worrin' about that stuff, boss. Not with me around."

"I'm sure of that." Then picking up his submachine gun, he said.

"Better check the grounds, boss. Make sure no creeps are hidin' or sneakin' around out there, with some fool plan to jump us." I nodded.

The moment Bernie stepped outside, I entertained the thought that perhaps his presence was going to be the only thing keeping me from meeting the same fate Chris and Meredith had.

"Damn those hit men! Damn them to hell!" My rant came to an abrupt end. The drowsy feeling was back, and it came quickly. I barely had time to stumble onto the sofa, before falling fast to sleep, and dreaming.

CHAPTER 6

I WAS NONE TOO PLEASED with Cyd's radiant smile when he greeted me.

"What am I doing back in this stupid dream?!"

"Could be your day, Bob." Without another word, we were floating off toward the oasis where Pleasant was waiting, and once again roasting those strange meatballs over a fire by the edge of the pool. Cyd vanished, and with the anger I'd brought with me into the dream, I scowled at Pleasant.

"What am I doing here? I told you I wanted no more of this. No more of this nonsense, and no more of you!" Pleasant looked up at me with his ingratiating smile, and said, "But, Bob, you lied to me. You told me you were not a killer, then in grand fashion you go and kill Carl."

"That was self-defense."

"Yes, but is that any different from what Frank asks of you?" Pleasant challenged. "Is killing to save the lives of your friends not also self-defense?"

"But what Frank asks of me is an impossible feat!"

"Yes, that would be a fool's folly, without help."

"The only folly is this dream. But now that I'm here again, you already know the only thing I want is to speak with Gloria's spirit."

"Now is that not timely?" Pleasant grinned.

"It just so happens I have spoken to Nice on this matter, and now that you've shown you are a killer, Nice will compromise regarding Gloria's spirit." I felt an immediate rush.

"I can see and speak to Gloria's spirit in this dream?"

"Perhaps," Pleasant smiled.

"It depends on what you will do. But before discussing it, let us share a meal together, bond our fellowship." If sharing a meal with him was what it took to see and speak to Gloria's spirit, I was ready to gorge myself.

"Let's eat," I smiled. As before, using our fingers, we sat, side-by-side, eating the strange-looking meatballs with gusto. Once again, a feeling of euphoria flooded my senses.

"Where's my drink?" I asked, and a goblet of that bubbly, champagne-looking liquid popped into my waiting hand.

"This time drink it," Pleasant smiled.

I raised the goblet in a merry salute to Pleasant, then swallowed the fizzy liquid in one gulp. The goblet vanished, and I felt my spirits rise along with a vitality and vigor that caused a wide grin to spread across my face.

"So, how is the illustrious Bernie doing in his endeavor of guarding you?" I felt giddy and couldn't stop myself from letting out a giggle in response. In that moment, the question was the funniest I'd ever heard.

"Swell as hell," I said. Then I giggled again. "Quite the comedy!"

"Marvelous, is it not?" Pleasant said also bursting into a fit of laughter.

"This entire business of hit men is so damn funny!" I roared with laughter now.

"It is funnier than you think. You are such a riot, Bob! Is it not delightful how everything is going to hell for you?"

There we were, two adult men, our bodies doubled over, roaring with laughter, tears in our eyes and lying back on the lush grass after losing our balance. And then the laughter subsided. All became quiet.

After a few moments Pleasant addressed me in a more serious tone, "Now that we have bonded in fellowship, it is time for us to talk." We both sat up, like two drunkards now sober enough to face the inevitable. Pleasant looked out over the water before addressing me.

"Bob, for you to see and speak to Gloria's spirit, this is what Nice... what I... want you to do. You must accept the mission Frank has entrusted you with. You must save the Fraternity and put an end to the murder of its members. You must put an end to the Cyprus Group."

"But...?" Pleasant gently raised a finger, showing I was to remain silent.

"As I have told you, you cannot comprehend the what and the why of what we do here. It is also futile for you to carry out what Frank has asked of you, without help. We will give you the help you need to successfully carryout your mission. Does this arrangement meet with your favor?"

"Before I take on this mission and accept your help, do I first get to see and speak with Gloria's spirit, in this dream?"

"You have a choice to make. You can choose not to take on the mission and accept our help, and let matters stand as they are now, and Nice will allow you to see Gloria's spirit, in this dream, but only for fleeting seconds. OR, you can accept the mission Frank has offered you, and our help, and I will see to it you can be with and speak to Gloria's spirit later, for an extended period. Which shall it be?"

"I want more than fleeting seconds with Gloria's spirit. Your word on that second deal?" God, what am I saying? Pleasant seems so real... everything seems so real that it's sucking me in. But this is only a dream and I'm encouraging this silly talk. I have to stop dreaming and get the hell out of here!

"Yes, my word," Pleasant responded.

This dream is so full of shit that to wade through it would even baffle Freud. I just want out of it! I'll never get to see Gloria's spirit here. Pleasant is nothing but double-talk. I just have to say what Pleasant wants me to say and end this dream.

"You seemed puzzled, Bob. Need time to think on it?"

"No, I'll take the deal with your help."

"Splendid!"

"Now can I go? Wake from this dream?"

"Cyd will escort you to your awakening point."

"Escort me? Why can't I just wake up now?" Pleasant gave me that gracious smile.

"You will see." Cyd appeared. We floated across the desert toward the dream's starting point, and once there, a scroll appeared in Cyd's hands. He looked at me, still smiling his captivating smile.

"This scroll contains a list of all Cyprus Group members."

This damn dream just wouldn't let go. "Why are you telling me this?"

"It also lists the addresses where you can find them alone on Friday, one week from tomorrow. Except for security people on that day, we will ensure family, friends, domestic help, and neighbors are not with them. We will disable internal and external security cameras. You take care of the live security, and the Cyprus Group members will be, as you mortals like to say, ready to get whacked!" He extended his hand to me.

"Take it."

"Oh, no! I've had enough for one dream. You can keep it." I sensed Cyd's radiant warmth cooling a bit.

"Pleasant will be mighty upset with me if you don't take it. Not to mention you." This was becoming too much.

"Will taking the scroll end this dream? This nonsense?"

"Yes."

I let out an exasperated sigh.

"Ah, hell! It better." I took the scroll from his hand. It felt weightless, and had the similar texture, shape and size of a papyrus.

"Copy its contents quickly. The scroll will vanish within minutes after it is unrolled."

"Are you out of your mind?!" Those were my last words before the dream ended.

I awoke, sprawled out on the sofa, and defying all measure of reality, in my right hand was the scroll Cyd had given me in the dream. I must be hallucinating. I blinked several times, praying the scroll would disappear. It didn't. The scroll was real, I could feel its texture against my fingers. How can this be possible? It was only a dream. I remembered Cyd's words and sat up.

"Copy the contents quickly. The scroll will vanish within minutes after it is unrolled." I leapt off the sofa, scroll in hand, and moved over to a desk where a large, yellow legal notepad and felt-tip pen rested on top of it. I sat down and carefully unrolled the scroll which revealed a three-page, typed document in English, plus a fourth page, but that one was blank. I transcribed the scroll's content onto the notepad as quickly as I could.

Then on the blank page, photos appeared with the addresses associated with them. The photos were mostly pairs of men and women. Husbands and wives. Other photos were of just one person, but all of them were members of the Cyprus Group. All of them the intended targets.

Using the camera on my smart phone, I tried to keep my hands steady as I snapped pictures of all the photos. Only seconds after taking the last photo, the scroll vanished. I looked over the information I had copied. The addresses were in 24 U.S. cities in four Time Zones.

In the Eastern Time Zone, eight cities: New York, Boston, Philadelphia, Washington, D.C., Pittsburg, Detroit, Atlanta and Miami. In the Central Time Zone, seven cities: Chicago, Minneapolis, St. Louis, New Orleans, Houston, Dallas and Corpus Christi. In the Mountain Time Zone, three cities: Denver, Phoenix and Tucson. In the Pacific Time Zone, six cities: Las Vegas, Los Angeles, San Francisco, San Diego, Portland and Seattle. A chill ran up my spine as I realized for the first time, Pleasant and Cyd are real!

It wasn't just a silly dream; I had struck a deal with the Gods of Winter. I didn't dare to imagine what would happen to me if I didn't follow through.

I felt trapped. And yet the deal I made was about trading something for something. Having access to the information in that scroll meant I was playing in the kill-or-be-killed game, something I did not want. But if I succeeded, they would grant me access to Gloria's spirit, something I wanted. But what were the odds of succeeding? There was the rub.

I would have to rely on my instincts. Let them

guide me. While my mind was at work on the makings of a viable plan, Bernie strolled back into the house to report on his outside inspection, the sub-machine gun still at the ready.

"Everything lookin' okay outside, boss. Scared off a deer and some critters." Bernie paused and said, "I was thinkin' maybe I should take the first shift later tonight boss."

"We'll be out of here well before then," I said.

CHAPTER 7

"**ALRIGHT!**" Frank beamed.

"I knew that assassin's bungled attempt on your life would clear your thinking... rip you out from under the rock you've been hiding under. I knew it! I knew it!"

"Wait a minute, hold on now, I'll accept only on one condition. I want total control of our operation from this moment on. That means without interference from anyone, and that includes you, Frank. I run the entire show from start to finish. Everyone follows my plan to the letter without question. That's how it's got to be if you want me onboard." I was talking to Frank on the cloned mobile Dave left me and I felt my mind was sharp and focused as I waited for Frank to respond.

"One more thing, no questions. Do you agree with these terms Frank?"

"You're damn right I agree! We're stumbling around in a hopeless fog without you."

"Okay, we have a deal. By the time they fly Bernie and me to Ann Arbor, I want you to have gathered all the members. I'll address them when I get there."

"I've already done that," Frank said.

"They're all under guard."

"Good. As soon as I land, I want you to have arranged some out-of-way place we can drive to straight from the airport. We need to discuss my plan privately."

"Consider it done!"

"One more thing, Frank. And this is the most important thing. We will need an isolated place, one furnished with modern conveniences, and with enough guards for protection. A place large enough to accommodate all the members in safety, and from there we can launch our operations against the Cyprus Group. We'll also need an airstrip that can handle our fleet of jets, plus additional land we can convert into a small combat obstacle training course and shooting range with lights."

"Christ, Bob, you're asking for the moon!"

"Then give it to me. You remember that villa which you loved so much? The one with the secluded lake?"

"How can I forget?"

"Well, it's still on the market. They're asking for a lot, but it will fill the bill. Buy it!"

"Bob, you are talking a lot money!"

"The fraternity can afford it. Now, no grumbling, Buy it! That's an order!"

"Okay, then. I'll get on it!"

"Get on to it right now. I want that place purchased and ready to move into today."

"But it will take time. What about attorneys?"

"Make moving in today a condition of the sale, Frank," I interrupted.

"They're in a hurry to sell. Use your influence, your irresistible charm, whatever it takes, but just make sure we can move in there today. We can do the closing with the attorneys later."

"Okay. I may have to resort to what I don't want to."

"Welcome to the club!" When the Lear jet landed on a private airstrip just outside of Ann Arbor, Michigan, Frank, dressed in casual clothes, met us with his 'ace' personal guard, Clyde Boreanaz, a tall, grim-looking hefty man with eyes like daggers and a bushy mustache.

Bernie and I deplaned, and the four of us got into an unimpressive old Chevrolet sedan. Clyde slid behind the wheel, Bernie squeezed himself in the front passenger seat beside him, the two looking like gorillas on holiday, while Frank and I sat in the back seat.

The out-of-the-way place Frank selected for our private meeting was a shabby diner in an old neighborhood where we wouldn't have to worry about eavesdropping. The diner was not all that inviting. It was the sort of place aiming to impress but missed the mark entirely with its bright, gaudy colors and shiny chrome trimmings. We chose two booths away from the other patrons.

Frank and I sat in one of the booths, across from one another. Bernie and Clyde in the one just behind us where the window offered an unobstructed view of the parking lot. We instructed them to keep their eyes open for anything unusual, and to be at the ready should there be a need to reach for their concealed weapons.

A young, bouncy waitress wearing an orange uniform matching the loud décor approached us. She had frosted hair, very blue eyes, and a narrow sun-wrinkled face.

"Hiya, I'm Jenny," she said and snapped her chewing gum before her mouth stretched into a crimson line meant to be a genuine smile.

"My, we don't usually get gents in here lookin' so handsome as you two," she said before leaning toward me, and revealing an uplift and separation of her breasts.

"Not with darlin' eyes like yours," she winked at me.

"Whatcha havin', hon?" I shot her a grave look and a weak smile.

"What darlin' eyes wants, is a little privacy, and whatever special you're serving today."

"Uh...yes, sir!"

"The same for my friend. And the two in the next booth. Take your sweet time." Frank's look of expectation let me know it was time to get to business.

"That villa we discussed... is it ready for us to move in?" I said.

"Yes, God damn strings you made me pull, but yes!"

"Good. Now, we need to clear some land for an airstrip and that will require extra guards, preferably with some construction experience. Also, some construction equipment to build out the airfield and combat training course. The work needs to begin immediately." Frank nodded.

I reached into the small briefcase I'd brought with me and pulled out a sheet of paper and placed it on Frank's side of the table.

"These are the names of all the members of the Cyprus Group, and their locations for this coming Friday."

"What?!" Frank exclaimed. "Where did you get these?"

"I got these names and addresses from the most reliable source possible."

"But Bob, if this information is accurate, how did you get it and so quickly?"

"Remember, no questions."

"Just like that? You expect me to accept this on faith?" I gave him a hard look, my eyes digging into him.

"If you don't accept it, you've broken our deal and I'm out of here. Finished with this mess. You're on your own."

"No, hold on, wait. We can't stop! You can't quit! Forget what I said."

"No more questions?"

"None!"

"You and the members will do whatever I ask and rely on it?"

"Yes. It's your show. You're in command. I'm not breaking our deal."

"Okay, let's get on with it. I'll need to know which of our guards have a military background, especially combat experience."

"Clyde's the only one with military combat experience, awarded combat medals too."

"I'll need a personal staff. Dave will be my chief aide, Bernie will coordinate all the guard activities. What I don't have is a personal secretary, someone from whom I can expect loyalty and hold in trust."

"Know of anyone that fits the bill, Frank?"

"I can have you meet some people."

"No time for that. Tonight, after I address the members, send me the candidate you feel is most suitable."

"You are rather discerning Bob. What if the person I dig up doesn't meet with your approval?"

"Then Dave will have extra work." At that moment our waitress arrived, balancing a large tray. The Day's Special turned out to be nachos, red and green salsa, pinto beans, tomatoes and jalapeno peppers. She set down two plates and two cups of hot coffee on each table.

"Ah, just a moment," I said. "I'll pay the check now." I pulled the cash out of my wallet to cover the check and then handed her a one-hundred-dollar bill.

"That's your tip for allowing us some privacy." Jenny stared down at the bill, her blue eyes wide as if she'd just won the lottery.

"Oh, my Lord! Oh, my!" she shrieked. "Oh, thank you, thank you! God bless you."

"I'm counting on it," I smiled. When we finished eating and rose from our booths, I said to Bernie, "You keep mum on everything you've overheard."

"Yes, boss,"

"That goes for you too, Clyde."

"Yes, boss." As we left the diner, Jenny, smiling effusively, waved to me.

I waved back.

CHAPTER 8

53 MEMBERS OF THE FRATERNITY, 37 men and 16 women, ranging in age from 29 to 69, all Caucasian save for one Asian and six African Americans were still alive and safely under guard at a safehouse. Ben Winters was still in the hospital with a slightly improving prognosis, and also still under guard.

When we arrived at the safe-house, Clyde and Bernie led us inside and after making our way through the foyer saw Dave who in Frank's absence had the near impossible task of keeping Fraternity members calm.

Dave was out of breath and looked flustered when he approached. His fiancée Kym, an attractive, petite brunette with bright hazel eyes and the youngest member at 29, was close at his heels.

"Bob?!" Dave exclaimed. He gave me a look that expressed both his surprise and delight.

"Bob's with us now," Frank said, with a satisfied look on his face. Dave knew how hard he'd been trying to convince me to accept this mission.

"Well, thank heavens!" Dave grinned and pulled me into a tight hug and gave me a firm clap on the back. Kym, looking less spirited yet also relieved, also pulled me into an embrace. When she pulled away from me I noticed the look of dread in her eyes.

"Will you take care of us? Take care of Dave?"

"I sure as hell will try, Kym." I said before turning my attention back to Dave.

"How are they looking, Dave?"

"They're spooked, Bob, walking around like God-damned ghosts, some of them."

"Let's put some life into 'em," I said.

"Kym, help Dave round 'em up, I need everybody in one room." Frank and I made our way into the living room and took our positions by a baby grand piano. We looked out at the sea of anxious faces. Some were standing, some pacing, others seated on chairs and sofas. In his inimitable style, and with an encouraging smile, Frank addressed the group.

"I know many of you want answers. You're concerned about your safety and you want to get back to your lives. Tonight, I have some important news to share with you." Frank's words elicited a few murmurs.

"We have all agreed," Frank continued, "that if Doctor Robert Daniels… Bob here… would lend us his talents, we would follow his lead. Bob knows how we can wipe out the Cyprus Group and eliminate the threat we're facing. He has accepted this mission and has vowed to do everything in his power to protect all of you." Despite the growing spread of murmurs and the louder din of other voices, Frank had every member's full attention.

"Therefore," Frank continued, "until we successfully wipe out this scourge, and it will come soon enough, I am turning my reign of authority over to Bob. This means that each of you, me included, will obey all of his commands without question. This applies to guards and all non-Fraternity help we receive."

His eyes now more alive, his voice more resounding, Frank asked, "Can you all abide by that?" Replies of approval flooded the room.

"So be it!" Frank beamed. "I now turn the floor over to your leader, Bob Daniels." All the members rose to their feet. The looks on their faces a mix of relief, hope and admiration. Bound by the oath of our Fraternity, they needed to know there was a way out of our shared dilemma. Their response moved me, but I was all too aware that this outpouring was premature. I needed to give them hope but ensure that no one let their guard down. With a stern expression on my face I took the floor and looked into each of their faces as I delivered what I knew they needed to hear.

"Make no mistake, we are embarking upon a challenging mission. Many of you will face the greatest test of your lives. I will call upon you to think, act and behave in the only way that can save your life. More will die. My mission is to ensure that it won't be anyone standing in this room." The murmurs quieted. I had their undivided attention.

"So please, listen carefully. We are at war! We will kill many people. Kill every member of the Cyprus Group. To win this war, we have to be as ruthless as they are. We need to set aside our altruistic nobility to save our own lives and the lives of other innocent people." I gave them a moment to take it all in. Kym, as I expected, was the most negatively affected by my words. The blood had drained from her face. The others wore a mix of uneasy trepidation.

"I need all of you backing me," I stressed. "Not one of you can fall apart on me." Then with my hands outstretched, my voice several octaves louder, I asked,

"Are you all with me on this?!" Kym was the first to express herself, her voice tremulous.

"Do we have to resort to killing?"

"Yes, unless you want to remain locked up in this safe-house for the rest of your life, hoping that a hit man doesn't slip through the guards outside and puts a bullet through your head!" I knew it was a harsh statement, the second I set it, but it's the only way to ensure they all understand what we're up against.

"Ladies and gentlemen, this is a kill-or-be-killed situation!"

"If we have no choice, killing is better than hiding for the rest of our lives," a member voiced. At that, others chimed in.

"I'm with that."

"I agreed to follow you... no matter what!"

"I'm with you."

"It's our time of reckoning!"

"Kill the bastards! Enough is, enough!"

"Let's do this!"

"We are honor-bound to support you."

"If you know a way forward, let's go Bob!"

"God save our souls, but I'm behind whatever you feel we must do."

"Is there anyone who will not stand behind me on this?" Silence.

"Okay," I said.

"You are all on a need-to-know basis. What you need to know now is that next Friday is the day we carry out our attack on the Cyprus Group. There is precious little time to waste. Frank has secured a location of absolute safety. We will move all of you there tonight. Spouses and family members cannot accompany you, however they will be under our security until after Friday, when this ordeal will be behind us. Private jets will fly you to the nearest commercial airport and private vehicles will transport you the rest of the way." I could sense the thought of leaving the safe-house put them instantly on edge.

"No time for heavy packing. Most everything you need will be available to you and flown in by air. Frank and Dave will hand out travel itineraries. Let's get a move-on!" As the members scrambled to get their travel itineraries, Dave rushed up to me, looking beside himself.

"Bob, I'm concerned about Kym. We both know she's not cut out for this kind of situation. She won't handle it well! And I can't bear to see her go through this kind of emotional anguish."

"Dave, from this moment forward you're my chief aide, what do you propose I do? We're dealing with life and death!" His look was pleading. "All I'm asking is that you keep her out of this as much as possible. I need to give her an assurance, calm her down. You have my word I'll back you every step of the way, please Bob." I took a moment before responding.

"Okay, I owe you, Dave. I will hold Kym as a reserve in anything directly having to do with the killings. But this is a heartless endeavor, and if push comes to shove, I, we can't play favorites."

"Understood, thanks Bob."

"Now let's move these people out of here, Frank needs your help with those travel itineraries." No sooner had Dave left to assist Frank when I noticed a beautiful woman strutting in my direction. She appeared to be in her late 30s, about five-foot-seven, and had what appeared to be a firm, flawless figure beneath a fitted white blouse, and blue slacks. Poised and with a reserved air of dignity, she was God damn stunning! Too stunning. No, she won't do at all.

I watched her approach so I could take in the loveliness of her angular face, her golden tanned skin, her full sensuous mouth, startling brown eyes, and the spill of shoulder-length reddish-gold of her hair. She doesn't belong here, or with me. What the hell was Frank thinking? Then her fragrant, honeysuckle aroma was upon me.

"Doctor Daniels?" she asked.

"Yes, and who might you be?"

"Susan Bishop." She said.

"Doctor Worsly informed me you are looking to hire a personal secretary."

"I've been expecting you," I said, extending my right hand out in greeting. As we shook hands, I noticed her gentle touch.

"Please, call me Bob."

"Please call me Sue," she smiled, with a hint of innocence I found disarming.

"Is there anything you'd like to know to ensure I'm the best fit for the post?"

I had already made my decision and found myself unable to resist asking, "Are you married... or engaged?"

"No, neither." That seemed impossible to believe. "You have no significant other or close friend whom you need to inform about your whereabouts? No one can know your location." She smiled, as if sensing my interest in her might be more than just professional.

"No, no one."

"This week, Sue, I'm involved in the war business. Being my personal secretary could be rough going... you will have to put up with harsh circumstances... maybe even dangerous ones."

"I am aware of that. I heard everything you said."

"And none of it bothers you?"

"No. As long as I don't have to kill anyone. I am sympathetic to your cause." Then both beautiful and intelligent, she added, "Survival has a certain nobility to it, don't you agree?"

"Did Frank put you up to that?"

"No one did," She said, then feigning offense smiled once again and which made the warmth return to her eyes. That got to me. Oh, the hell with it, I thought. I have to get moving. I sighed, then said, "You're hired. We have to get out of here and you'll be flying with me. I'll explain more about what you'll be doing when we get on the jet."

CHAPTER 9

ON SATURDAY AT DAWN we arrived at the place Frank purchased, a villa located 86 miles from the nearest commercial airport. The perfect place for a relaxing getaway. Today it would become a combat training facility.

Trucks carrying materials and construction equipment detoured through a service road. The caravan of rented vehicles transporting Fraternity members made their way through large stone pillars that marked the paved drive toward the entrance. There were acres of manicured grounds all along the sloping roadway that led to a majestic iron gate with curved railings on both sides.

A winding, cobbled driveway that brought the villa into view was flat and led to a lake surrounded by a vast verdant lawn covered in eucalyptus and Camellia shrubs. The tall growth of white oaks and pines made for an almost windless climate.

The villa itself had a magnificent courtyard with a bubbling granite fountain at its center. And just beyond it, you could see a primrose yellow Mediterranean stucco structure four stories high, with white balconies and porches. Large double mahogany doors complimented the red-tiled roof.

You couldn't help feel the place held some kind of enchantment especially with the way the early morning light colored the gardens and all its surroundings.

Inside, the first three floors of the villa were lavishly furnished. I had the members assembled in the sunken living room which had a vaulted ceiling and at its center a five-tier crystal chandelier. Long, ivory silk draperies framed the floor to ceiling windows. The polished oak floor was covered in carefully placed Aubusson rugs in muted colors. The armchairs were upholstered in heavy white silk and the sofas in green leaf velvet. A black baby grand piano sat at one end of the room. Along the walls, fine impressionist paintings, gilded antique mirrors and a tall glass display case containing a valuable collection of figurines. Throughout were Galle curved lamps, large vases of daffodils and peonies, and marquetry tables displaying sculptures and rare objects of art.

Despite the exquisite surroundings I was cognizant of the fact that all the members were as tired from the journey as I was, and I'd need to keep my address to them short.

"Everyone, grab six hours of sleep, then return here. Your sleeping quarters are on the second and third floors. Frank will pass out your room assignments. Rest assured you will be greeted by the ultimate in comfort.

The guards had already been given their room assignments on the fourth floor, along with a schedule for when they would be trading shifts. This ensured there was always someone manning a post both inside and outside the property. Bernie and Clyde's schedule mirrored mine and Frank's.

Four of the guards had culinary skills and were assigned to the state-of-the art kitchen where they were to begin meal preparation immediately. The two other groups of guards were charged with building out the airstrip and setting up the combat training range.

As the members scattered to get their room assignments, I pulled Sue to the side.

"We have adjoining rooms on the second floor. I'm always working, so I'll need you close by, to keep on top of what I'm doing."

"Understood," she said and then smiled. She certainly seemed eager to please.

Carrying my briefcase, I led her up a magnificently curving staircase to the second floor, where we proceeded down a corridor before stopping by the door of my room. I opened the door to the tranquil ambience of a large, luxurious room with silk-draped, floor-length windows and a sliding glass door providing a spectacular view of the lake.

"Oh, how breathtaking!" Sue marveled, following me into the room.

"You'll find your accommodations are like mine." I watched Sue's expression of delight as she took in every detail. The Caribbean folk art paintings lining the walls. The five-light chandelier made from the natural wash of pink, brown, orange and ivory seashells. A king-size bed in the far corner with a matching matted rush headboard and bench. A pale blue bedspread that tastefully complemented the silk window drapes. Walnut wood nightstands on each side of the bed, the one closest to us had an in-house telephone and hand painted porcelain lamp resting upon it.

The carpeting was honey wheat, and scattered about were houseplants in unglazed terracotta pots, a curved settee, a walnut dresser, and a couple of small tables with pale blue silk cloths on which set flower vases and table lamps, and a large walk-in wardrobe.

Looking into the empty wardrobe, I commented, "This shouldn't be empty for long. Frank is flying in sufficient clothing for everyone once the air strip's ready."

A humorous glint made its way through the radiant flecks of Sue's lovely brown eyes.

"I can't wait for my dancing gown," she said facetiously. That warmth again.

"Too bad you'll be dancing on the edge," I said. Sue followed me through an alcove leading from the bedroom to a small kitchenette, which led to a Roman-style sunken bathtub with gold fittings. Two small passageways, one leading to a glass encased showering area, the other to a long ivory sink and matching commode.

"Wow, this room... the entire villa," Sue exclaimed in breathless amazement, "must have cost someone a fortune!"

"Yes... the Fraternity. Not much petty cash left now." We made our way back into the main room, where I opened the door adjoining Sue's room with mine. I took a peek inside and noticed the only difference was the color scheme.

"You like it?" I asked, boss-like, but my voice more emotive.

"I love it!" Sue beamed. "Thank you!"

"Thank the Fraternity." Then placing my hand on the door knob, I said, "Look, you can lock the door from your side when you need some privacy, and just in case I walk in my sleep."

"Okay."

"Get some sleep, that's an order!"

"Yes, boss."

"And quit addressing me like Bernie does. You can still call me Bob." I slept only three of the six hours before I found myself at the desk in my room. The contents from my briefcase spread out before me.

My biggest concern was getting the airstrip finished so it could handle our fleet of Lear jets. Some work on the airstrip had begun before we arrived, but from the feedback I'd gotten so far, things were slow, too slow and that could prove to be a big headache. The combat range was also delayed.

The next priority was assembling the assault teams and air groups. I needed 24 members in each. Frank, Dave and I would be handling the Command Center, so that left me with 49 members. I began working back and forth, putting together a list of the

24 I felt were best suited for the assault teams. That left me with 25 members for the air groups. But I only needed 24, leaving me with one extra member I could hold in reserve.

Thinking back to the conversation with Dave, I knew Kym was the best to hold on reserve. That would put both their minds at ease and ensure Dave would be free of emotional distractions which could compromise our mission.

Twenty minutes before I was scheduled to address the members, I was pouring over background information on the guards. Many of them lacked military training, what I most wanted.

The door to Sue's adjoining room opened, and she entered carrying a silver tray. As usual, she greeted me with that radiant smile of hers.

"Thought you could use a fresh cup of coffee to perk you up."

I glanced up at her in surprise.

"Thank you, you didn't have to do that."

"I know. Consider it a bonus... for not sleepwalking."

When I was back in the living room, I looked around at the anxious faces. I knew we were on the clock and I had to contain whatever reservations I had up until that point. I stood in the center of the sunken living room where Frank had set up the board I'd requested. After a few moments I could tell everyone was ready for me to begin.

"I need to speak with each of you privately. Each

member's name is listed on this board along with the scheduled meeting time." I extended my right arm to draw their attention to it.

"In the dining room, you will find a buffet, please help yourselves to something to eat while these member meetings are in session." Kym was the last on the schedule. My decision to make her the reserve member meant I needed to take a different approach. I couldn't have the same conversation with Kym I had had with the others.

"I'm putting you on emergency reserve, meaning you will have nothing to do with what I'm asking of the others, nor will you have to take part in their discussions. You set your own course, doing what you feel comfortable doing. Just make no objections. And do not interfere, especially with Dave. They will be involved in what is critical to our objective."

"Can you accept those conditions?" Kym let out a sigh of relief.

"Yes. Yes, of course. Thank you, Bob!" The one-on-one meeting with the members done meant it was time to call a meeting with my personal staff, Dave, Bernie and Sue.

My office was set up in the library, which had a subdued atmosphere and was more like an English gentleman's club complete with floor-to-ceiling bookcases and a marble fireplace.

When I entered the room, Dave was sitting on the sofa, Bernie in an armchair, and Sue behind the desk, notepad and pen at the ready. Clyde whom I summoned to this meeting was standing near a smaller desk in the corner.

My expression reflecting that time was of the essence, I said to Dave, "I want you to leave right now and check on the progress the guards are making in constructing the airstrip. From now on, that's your added responsibility. See what you can do to get their slow asses moving. Also, while you're there, check in on the progress the other guards are making with the combat training obstacle course and shooting range." Once Dave had closed the door behind him I turned to Clyde and handed him a sheet of paper.

"Aside from you and Bernie, this is a list of the twenty-four guards whom I feel will best serve as our killers on the assault teams. I want you to round them up and take them to whatever exists of our combat training obstacle course and shooting range. You know what I need you to do with them, using your military experience to do it. Push them hard. Every day, morning and afternoon. You can start right now." Clyde grinned. "Sure thing, boss. But for that I'll need some rifles... pistols... ammunition. Maybe some knives."

"Take a look in the gun room. I'll provide you what you really need once the airstrip is ready and the weaponry can be flown in. Get moving!"

"Gotcha, boss."

Then it was time to address Bernie.

"I understand from studying your background

that you were an aide in some kind of ROTC training."

"Yeah, boss, before bein' kicked out of college for crackin' skulls."

"Here's what I need from you. There are twenty-four members Frank is assembling for me, the Fraternity halves of the assault teams, each of whom will be teamed up with one of the guard killers Clyde is training. I want you to whip those members into shape for me on the training course." A slow, devilish-like grin eased over Bernie's face.

"How rough you want me to be on 'em, boss?"

"Nothing overly strenuous. Most of these members are not in peak physical condition. This is to be more mental than physical, instilling in them a military mindset of oneness and discipline. They need to acquire mental combat readiness. Do some light drills... some marching... calisthenics... target practice. Give them short breaks. Put them through this kind of workout every day, starting today."

"Is this something you can do, Bernie?"

"Sure, boss."

"Good. See what's in the gun room. Frank should have these members waiting for you, so get to it!"

"Yeah, boss."

"Oh and steer clear of Clyde, he'll be training the guards out there too."

Bernie nodded, then left. When we were alone, Sue spoke.

"Bob, the members... they don't seem capable of

withstanding the training you've prescribed. If it would be helpful, I'm willing to train too. I could be your backup."

"Your duties don't require that," I said. "Just stick to what I've outlined for you. Secretarial functions, keeping records of those coming in and out of here, and keeping on top of what Bernie, Clyde, even Dave and Frank, are up to help me coordinate their activities when needed. Lastly, bringing to my attention anything you feel is vitally important."

"Whatever I can do to be of help," Sue smiled. Damn that smile! Get a grip! I reprimanded myself.

Dave got back to me by early afternoon.

"The guards detailed at the airstrip are moving way too slow and not getting much done. Hell, most of them have no idea how to handle a bulldozer."

"Take me there. Let me see," I said. Arriving at the airstrip site, I saw that what Dave had told me was correct. Distressed, I spoke to the guard foreman, Hank, a big fellow in charge.

"Your progress here is terrible and we're way behind schedule! Look, Hank, we're in dire need of munitions and other critical supplies, and the only way we can get them is to fly them in. You damn well need to get on your people's asses, have them work faster, with much better results than this, or I'll damn well be kicking your ass!"

"Boss, these guys have never worked on a project like this one. We're doin' the best we can." I studied what was supposed to become an airstrip.

"You think there's any possibility that just one jet could land here right away?"

"It would take one hell of a pilot bent on suicide. I'd say it a take at least three more days of work before this strip is fit to handle jets landin'." I turned to Dave.

"We don't have three more days. We must have at least one jet able to land by tomorrow. Getting this airstrip ready for that, Dave, is your baby, so make it happen!"

"Hell, Bob, that would require me to bring in men and equipment from the outside more able to do this job and doing that would blow our secrecy. Is that what you want?" I could use a strong drink. I wrestled with the possibility of defeat creeping into my mind. What have I gotten myself into?

"No. Don't do that. Let me think on it," I said. Exhaustion and worry took over when I returned to my room very late that evening. Thankfully, Sue was asleep in her room, sparing me from dealing with the warmth of her smile. I slumped onto my bed without undressing.

Early Sunday morning, shortly after I awakened, while sitting on the edge of my bed attempting to smooth away the wrinkles in my clothes, Sue entered my room, again carrying a hot fresh cup of coffee, but this time her smile absent. Setting the tray on the bed beside me, she looked down at me with a concerned expression, and said, "You mentioned that part of my duties was to tell you if anything alarmed me. Well, something is alarming me, you!" she said.

"You look haggard, so worn out you sleep in bed with your clothes on. You're trying to do too much!" I looked up at her wearily, a bit surprised.

"No one else can do it," I said.

"Well, today you take it easy. Let go of the stress you're putting on yourself."

"That an order?" I asked, finding her comment a bit amusing.

"No, a suggestion. One good piece of advice you should heed." I sighed.

"Okay… I'll try," I said, knowing it would be impossible for me to take it easy.

"Good, now drink your coffee," she said. "Relax, and I'll see you in your office. Everything will be fine." God, if only I could believe that.

Before heading back to the airstrip, I stopped by the combat training area. Like the airstrip, we were behind schedule and I desperately needed both to be completed as fast as possible if I had any hope of successfully carrying out my plan against Cyprus.

The morning sky was filled with patches of fog, which made me feel like some medieval ghost appearing out of a Scottish mist. I stopped, my eyes searched until I caught sight of them, Bernie breathing down the necks of his twenty-four Fraternity members like an impatient drill sergeant. He was putting them through their paces. I watched as they finished their ground calisthenics, then lined up single file with makeshift rifles as Bernie yelled at those who didn't do everything as he'd instructed.

"Let's go people! Move! Look alive!" Bernie yelled. "Left-right, left-right. Suck in that gut. Let's see some fire in 'em eyes!" The members were sweaty and exasperated, but they were not yet the feral beasts I wanted. They still lacked the fighting spirit needed for the battle to come.

Satisfied with Bernie's progress, I walked through another fog patch which opened onto a clearing. Clyde running drills with his guards, but no sooner had I arrived when Clyde jogged over to my side.

"Boss... boss, these guys are absolute wash-outs!" Clyde complained. "They may be great at guardin' people at close range, for what ya want me to teach 'em they're hopeless... lousy... the pits!"

"What?! Don't tell me that. Those are my killers out there!" Clyde shook his head.

"Not these guys, boss. They just don't have it in 'em. That special urge inside, to be able to learn and carry out that special way of killin' ya want. Not even close. No way. Ya'd never win yer war with this bunch. I know. A waste of time tryin' to make 'em into somethin' they can't be." Damn it! My plan was unraveling, and we hadn't even gotten all that far.

"What ya want me to do with them, boss?"

"Dismiss them. You're finished with them." I omitted to say that we all were finished.

CHAPTER 10

I WAS HEADING BACK INSIDE and making my way through the still thick patch of fog when the now familiar feeling of overwhelming drowsiness hit me.

I collapsed where I was and entered the dream.

I found Pleasant by the pool, his eyes studying me with amusement.

"What am I doing here?" I asked.

"I thought you could use some of these, what is it you call them? Meatballs?" He handed me a plate, but what he served me on it looked different. Less round and odorless.

"These are my specialty. They will help you."

"Help me?... How?"

"You need killers, do you not? A special kind." That cut through my daze.

"Yes. And I need them now!"

"Then eat your meatballs." I didn't know what he was up to, but I figured it couldn't hurt to eat something. I used my fingers and pushed the first one into my mouth and chewed. The taste was pungent but surprisingly invigorating. I swallowed and immediately felt better. I ate another and another until my plate was empty. I'm not sure what was in them, but

I did feel a lot better. I looked around, expecting company, but we were still alone.

"Where are my killers? You said…"

"They are not here," Pleasant gently interrupted. "You're going to need the Mafia." All I could manage was a dumb questioning look.

"The Mafia?! Why?"

"Because the Mafia has the killers you need and will give them to you."

"Are you crazy?! Why would the Mafia want to give me killers? I have no contact with the Mafia. I know nothing about them."

"But Cyd does. Cyd will help you, and so will the meatballs you ate." I didn't believe a word Pleasant said about the Mafia. It seemed too farfetched. I had no airstrip and no killers. Despair started to edge its way back into my mind.

"If I fail at my end of our deal, do I still get to see and speak to Gloria's spirit?"

"You will not fail! I am keeping my end of our deal, and you are keeping your end of it. Cyd will see to that." Pleasant vanished then and Cyd's tall, golden tanned figure appeared standing next to me.

"Delighted to see you again and be at your service." Cyd said.

"I see we have some matters requiring my special touch."

"The Mafia killers?" I asked.

"Yes. Rather pesky lot. But you should be able to persuade them to be your killers." Okay now neither

Pleasant or Cyd were making much sense to me.

"I see you have doubts about this," Cyd said and smiled.

"Look, this isn't funny! It's ludicrous, okay?! I don't know a single person in the Mafia, much less possess whatever it would take to entice them to help me."

"Now, Bob, just calm down, relax, and listen. Okay?" I stood there waiting, thinking he can't possibly have any idea how preposterous this all sounded.

"Abe Vocarro, is the chairman of the Mafia's let's call it, National Commission. He will provide you with your killers. Mafia killers."

"Why in hell would he do that?" I asked.

"Yes, forgive me. I suppose I am jumping ahead a little. What you need to know Bob is that the commission's top gun, known as the Red Baron, before his retirement, was used to eliminate whoever had incriminating evidence against top Mafia leaders. One of the Red Baron's hits, to use the mob's lingo, was whacking a mark, Franco Cortillino, in Detroit. Cortillino's testimony would have led to Voccaro rotting in a prison cell. Vocarro is therefore indebted to the Red Baron, a man he respects but also fears. Vocarro will give the Red Baron anything he wants." As fascinating as this tale was, I was still confused.

"Okay, but why are you telling me all of this about the Red Baron?"

"Because, Bob, the Red Barron's identity is a secret and since no one knows his true identity in the Mafia ranks, you will become the Red Baron."

"What?!"

Cyd smiled and waited for his words to sink in. "You see, what makes this possible is that dear Abe does not know, nor does anyone else, what the Red Baron looks or sounds like, which presents an opportunity for you to impersonate him. If you can deliver an Academy Award performance, then you can have Vocarro eating out of your hand and coughing up the hit-men killers you need. Neat, eh?"

"Academy Award performance?" The thought alone of coming face-to-face with Vocarro and Mafia killers left me cold. "I don't have the slightest idea how to relate to them," I said.

"And I sure as hell don't know how to contact them Cyd. And let's not forget they're not too friendly, they're vicious! Too damn vicious to control. You got the wrong man if you think I can control them."

"Perhaps I can be of some assistance."

A small goblet containing a blue-tinted liquid appeared in my right hand. The scent was intoxicating.

"What's this?" I asked.

"A little medicine, but it's tasty. Drink it." The lure of the liquid's aroma was irresistible. Without hesitation, I drank the sweet liquid in one long gulp. I waited a few moments.

"I don't feel any different. Am I supposed to?"

"You will feel its effects once you are face-to-face with Vocarro and his killers," Cyd said, a look of knowing flashing in his eyes.

"Bob, you are now capable of unimaginable feats

when you come into contact with members of the Mafia. You will be able to read their thoughts, and through your own words and thoughts you will be able to control them; instill fear in them to bring about what you command; even paralyze them and inflict pain if they get out of hand."

"That liquid I drank will allow me to do all of that?"

"Yes. To allow you to carry out your end of our deal. But once that is achieved, all of these gifts... your gifts...will disappear, and none from the Mafia with whom you come into contact will have any recollection of their association with you." Then a sheet of paper popped up in Cyd's hand with something written on it, and handing the paper to me, he said, "Here is Abe Vocarro's personal address in New York city. He will be there today, heavily guarded. Have a couple of your people fly up there and I will see to it that they encounter no resistance in picking him up and flying him to your location. This lack of resistance will also be the case for all the Mafia members Vocarro will be having your people pick up. I'll make certain that all comes off quickly and smoothly."

"Hold it!" I said. "There can't be any flying today. What airstrip we have at the villa is such a mess it's impossible for our jets to takeoff or land."

"I will remedy that immediately! You will be able to fly today. And while I'm at it, I will have your obstacle training course and firing range quickly brought up to snuff. After all, what are friends for?" He paused, flashed me a triumphant smile, then said, "Now go and do what must be done." His dark, keen eyes glowed with serenity.

"And Bob."

"Yes?"

"From here on in, you are on your own... until all the Cyprus Group members are killed." The dream abruptly ended.

I awakened to a world of improbabilities. In my hand I was holding the paper Cyd had given me in the dream, and I could recall every word he had spoken to me, as if I now had a photographic memory.

The fog had lifted, and as I slowly and calmly picked myself up from the ground, I could hear the sounds of new workmen and new equipment arriving on the obstacle training course and firing range, and beyond, similar sounds echoing from the airstrip, only more pronounced.

"Ya okay, boss?"

I didn't answer.

CHAPTER 11

SUNDAY MORNING brought everyone emotional upheaval. It all began shortly after I woke from my involuntary slumber and heard a commotion at the nearby work sites. I approached the airstrip and saw Dave, waving his arms wildly, and yelling out to me as he ran toward me.

"Bob... Bob!" He shouted.

"Something crazy has taken place... and... and I mean crazy! Right out of nowhere... these workmen... materials... equipment, they... they appeared, scaring the guards off, and... and with unbelievable speed, they finished the God-damned runway! Look! There's even a small control tower... a hangar... a fuel dump... everything! And Bob, after they finished, everything and everyone just vanished." Dave caught his breath. "Bob, what's going on here?"

"Hell if I know Dave." I couldn't suppress my smile thinking, Good show, Cyd.

"Look, whatever happened, getting in an uproar about it doesn't change it."

"But Bob don't you want to understand what happened?"

"No, I don't."

"But..."

"Dave, pull yourself together and get back to work, okay?"

"Jesus! Okay, okay." Just then a Learjet was descending onto the now finished airstrip.

"There will be other jets coming in later today with supplies. Have the pilot of this jet wait on the tarmac, ready to roll, and get Clyde into my office."

"All right. Just give me a moment to collect myself. Jesus." With word spreading about the bizarre happenings at the airstrip and obstacle course, Dave, with Clyde helping, pushed us past the members huddled anxiously outside my office. Everyone was in panic mode and wanted an explanation. I pulled Dave to the side.

"I need you to keep this mob under control. There's no time to explain, but we'll have a guest by the name of Vocarro later on today. I want you in the room with me when he gets here, and I need you to keep quiet unless I speak to you. Whatever you see or hear, remember, no questions. Wait here for Clyde, he'll be out in a few minutes. Got it?!"

"Okay, got it! Sure, whatever you need Bob." I motioned for Clyde to follow me into my office.

"Clyde, listen carefully. Calm down and stay on the alert."

"Uh... yes, boss."

"I need you to do something."

"Whatever you need, boss."

"What I need, and I need it pronto, is for you to fly to New York and pick up Abe Vocarro, a Mafia Padrone."

"Abe Vocarro?! The Abe Vocarro, the Mafia king-pin?! He's one vicious sonofabitch! I could never get close to 'im. Guy lives in a fort and its guarded like one." Clyde brought a hand to his chest, his composure starting to crumble.

"Boss, ya don't want me messing' with this guy. That would be... suicide."

"I don't want you messing with him, I want you to bring him to me," I said steadily, my eyes unfaltering.

"Ya want me dead Boss?!"

"Don't be melodramatic, Clyde. Besides, sonsabitches can be tamed. You'll see."

"You must trust me and believe you will meet with no resistance. I would not carelessly put your life, or anyone else's life, in danger." I walked over to the desk where Sue was taking notes and grabbed a sheet of paper.

"This is Abe Voccaro's home address. He's there now. Dave will escort you to the jet that will fly you to New York, take one of the other guards with you. Upon your return, bring Abe here to my office. Remember what I said and get moving!"

"Yes, boss!" I don't know if it was Pleasant's meatballs, or Cyd's drink, or both, but there was definitely something strange going on.

Once Dave and Clyde set off for the airstrip, Bernie had his hands full holding off the members outside, which left me alone with Sue.

"You're more charming that I thought," Sue said.

"Charm comes with the job."

"I can only imagine the hell Clyde is feeling in having to carry out your orders."

"Not as much hell as you think."

"Confronting Abe Vocarro sounds like a lot of hell to me. Even with your reassurances." I instinctively felt it was time to lighten the mood a little.

"This is an opportunity for Clyde to show off his tender side. Besides, it's always a great time to visit the big apple."

"I hope Vocarro shares your black humor," Sue said. Then she tried muffling a girlish giggle.

"He'll hear more of it when Clyde drags him in here," I grinned.

"You're convinced Clyde will succeed, aren't you?"

"Yes, Sue, I am." I smiled. "By the sound of it, there's still a mob outside my door. How about we use the private door and move this conversation to the Bar Room? There's something I'd like to discuss with you."

"I've heard that it's cozy in the Bar Room Dr. Daniels. Are your intentions honorable?" That smile and that tantalizing tease got to me.

"God help me if they aren't."

The Bar Room was empty. Sue was right, it was cozy with its sconce lighting, pine wood paneling and built-in bar. Red leather covered the service table and there were endless rows of wine and spirits. The lounge area where I wanted to sit with Sue had several cushioned-backed rosewood chairs, a carved rosewood pedestal table, and a wide brown velvet sofa complete with mocha pillows. I gently placed my right hand on the small of Sue's back and steered her toward the sofa.

"So far," I began, "I've only briefly spoken with Frank on this, and I'm trying to prepare Dave, but you also need to know what's going on. Before I address the members, we need to be in sync."

"Is it connected to what happened at the airstrip?"

"You might say that."

"Bob, what happened?"

"Your guess is as good as mine. But I'm thankful it did. We have more pressing matters and I will need your help in coordinating them." I paused, for a moment sidetracked with regret that I had to lie. There was an unexpected feeling of tenderness toward her. I noticed she was studying me. Was it possible she could sense I wasn't being straight with her?

"What is it you want to tell me Bob?"

"I've changed my plan. I Intended to use the guards as my killers, but that...that's proving to be impossible. In their place, I will rely on vicious Mafia hit men. I have to bring them here, and team them up with Fraternity members." Sue grabbed my arm, her fingers tightened their grip before she realized what she'd done and released me.

"Oh, forgive me... but Bob, first you want to bring Abe Vocarro here and now you're saying you want to bring his friends?! That's so, so unsettling. Are you sure?" I looked at her, a softness coming to my eyes.

"Now listen…" I started. But Sue wasn't listening.

"I just don't see how you're going to get the members to cooperate."

"Sue, I have no choice." Unable to stop herself, she grabbed my arm again, squeezed it tighter this time.

"But, how can you deal with the Mafia? They're brutal." She was getting emotional.

"If anything happened to you… " Gently, I broke her grip on my arm, placed my hands on her shoulders, and looked deeply into her eyes.

"Nothing will happen to me," I said. "I will control these Mafia killers. Don't ask me how, but it's built into my plan." She gave me an incredulous look.

"You… you're sure?"

"I'm certain." She unexpectedly threw her arms around my neck.

"That makes me feel better," she whispered. Emotions stirred in me that shouldn't have stirred. I felt her heart beating, and I reluctantly pulled myself away from her.

"I need for you to be brave, Sue."

"I will." Then she kissed me lightly on the cheek.

"Let's get back to the office." Fraternity members cycled in and out of my office for several hours. I did my best to allay their fears and give them a viable explanation for what they had seen or heard. Most walked away with the realization that regardless of how it happened, a jet could now land and deliver our much-needed supplies.

I had only a few moments to collect myself before

Clyde was back in my office with none other than Abe Vocarro, a middle-aged, balding, hot-tempered Italian with a rotisserie tan and a very bad attitude. He was about five-foot-eleven and dressed in an expertly tailored designer suit and expensive shoes. Looking into his lean face, I took in the beady eyes, the scar on his right cheek, his pronounced jaw and the hard line of his mouth and I knew this carnivore was ready to pounce.

"He's clean," Clyde said.

"Give you any trouble?" I asked.

"None, boss."

"Outstanding, Clyde. You can wait outside but stay close. I'll have another job for you. You'll be working in the Bar Room until further notice." Clyde nodded, then quickly left the room, leaving Sue, sitting uneasily behind her desk, Dave, sitting in a chair in the far corner, and our guest of honor directly across from me.

I turned my attention to Vocarro. It was time for my Academy Award performance.

"Enjoy your flight?" Vocarro glared at me.

"I damn well enjoyed nothing, and soon neither will you," he sneered.

"What's the goddamned meaning of snatching me out of my home? Do you know who the hell I am? It's your funeral! Your ass is history, man. All of you. Believe me, I'll remember you and this place." I leaned forward in my chair so he could get a better look at me.

"After I saved your miserable ass, this is how you speak to me? Threats? No one disrespects the Red Barron. I thought you knew that Abe."

"Red Baron, you?! "You lying bastard! Don't make me laugh."

"Franco Cortillino wasn't laughing either just before I whacked his ass in Detroit. As he found out, and you will too, I do not take threats, nor insults, lightly." I watched Vocarro change before my eyes. His entire demeanor morphing from bravado to fear.

"You planning to whack me?!"

"What do you think?"

"No, wait! Look, I'll do anything. Just... just don't..."

"Anything?" I said.

"Yes. Anything!"

"So, we have an understanding."

"Yes, yes. Okay. What do you want me to do?" In minutes I had Vocarro on the phone, urgently summoning twenty-four of the most vicious Mafia killers he knew and could locate who were not in jail or prison. I remained by the phone with him, listening over his shoulder, making certain he wasn't pulling a fast one and was connecting with the people I needed.

Cyd had said it would be quick and easy, and now it was happening. Vocarro handed me a list of the twenty-four associates and their whereabouts so we could pick them up and transport by jet to the villa. It was time to unveil the next phase of the plan to the members.

Both Sue and Dave had a look of bewilderment on their faces. I handed Dave a note.

"Call in all our jets and put Clyde in charge of this. Have him select guards he feels are up to the task and can bring every man on this list back here as quickly as possible. No questions." When Dave left, I sat back down across from Vocarro.

"I did what you asked, "you're not... you're not going to..."

"Blow your head off?" I cut through his words. As Cyd had told me, I could read his mind.

"No," I said. "I'm not through with you." Then something interesting happened. While I sat there silently watching Vocarro, I could hear his thoughts.

Your mistake. When my friends show up, I'm turning them loose on you. Make you crawl, you, sonofabitch, after they break your damn arms, legs and jaw.

I smiled at him.

"Abe. I hate to break it to you, but I don't enjoy crawling. Not good on the knees. Tell you what, why don't I break your arms, legs and jaw instead?"

Vocarro's mouth fell open.

"How? Hey, what are you?!"

"I'm what will use your head as target practice if you have any more bad thoughts about me." My words were so soft-spoken they terrified the hell out of him. I could see him struggling against his own mind.

"No, no, no. No more fucking bad thoughts."

"Now, you will remain in here until all your people

arrive," I said and paused to listen to Vocarro's mind, but I apparently had his full attention.

"Someone will keep you company in case you have any more of bad thoughts."

Vocarro put his face in his hands. He was looking desperate.

"Make yourself comfortable while you wait," I said, my tone suggesting that we were the best of friends.

"Cream in your coffee?" As Cyd told me, I now had complete control over Vocarro's movements whenever I needed it. I wouldn't put it past the Red Baron to poison my coffee, Vocarro thought.

"No Coffee," I'm fine," he said.

"I wouldn't poison you, Abe," I smiled.

"Lucky for you that thought didn't make it into the bad category." Merely using my thoughts, I could have put him in a paralyzed state, but that would complicate matters for now, so I let him be. At that moment, Rascal, a guard Clyde had recommended to me, came into the office, bearing, of all weapons, a submachine. I decided it was a good call.

"Keep him comfortable and see that he eats well. But see to it he stays put and stays quiet." Then, more for Vocarro's ear, I added, "If he tries to leave, or makes any disturbing noises, or in any way gets out of line, you have my permission to use his head as target practice, but don't mess up the paintings."

"Right, boss, you can count on that." Then with a fiendish-like grin showing he was enjoying the moment, Rascal pointed the muzzle of the submachine gun at Vocarro's head as a warning he had better behave, or else. The last thing I heard before leaving my office with Sue was the stifled screams inside Vocarro's mind.

"Bob, you scared me in there, I didn't expect you could be so threatening, especially to someone like Vocarro." I tried to hide my grin. "Quite a performance, wouldn't you say?"

"You mean that was just an act?"

"Just good PR for getting him to give me what I wanted."

"But what about this Red Barron business?"

"Nice guy," I said facetiously.

"He's got a killer resume." Then more seriously, "Sue, the Red Barron is a role I need to take on so this entire plan goes off as intended. Just accept it and try to relax."

"Relax? Bob, you just gave orders to that man to use Vocarro's head as target practice if he gets out of line!"

"Vocarro won't get out of line. Trust me. Now enough questions, I know what I'm doing. And beginning immediately my office is off limits to you. From now on you're working in the Bar Room until further notice."

CHAPTER 12

BY SUNDAY AT DUSK, the first of Vocarro's friends arrived. Vocarro, Dave and I were in the library when Clyde ushered in Roberto Giacolone, a brawny, 200 pound plus, brown-haired, red-faced mobster with a bushy mustache, and a face that looked as though a sledge-hammer had once kissed it. He wore casual clothes and looked like he was in his early 30s. Clyde pushed him into a chair directly across from Vocarro and I could tell from the cold, menacing stare he was none too pleased about being summoned. Vocarro was the first to speak.

"Roberto! Long time," he said. Giacalone flexed his broad shoulders, twisted his neck and body, rotated his forearm and wrist muscles, and didn't smile.

"Who was that guy? Treated me like shit."

Vocarro's smile didn't waver. "Careful, Roberto."

"Well, what the hell's so urgent? Anyone else but you I wouldn't give 'im the time. This damn well better be worth it."

"To me it is," Vocarro said, his smile diminishing.

"Roberto, I'd like you to meet someone." He gestured a hand toward me.

"Someone you know by reputation, the Red Baron." Something in Giacalone's face shifted, a mix of fear and surprise. And just like with Vocarro, I could read his mind. Shit! This is a God-damn setup? Giacalone mused.

"Abe, hell," Giacalone grunted, jumping to his feet.

"What I ever do to you?" He attempted to reach for a weapon, but his arms were so heavy he couldn't.

"Hey, what's going on?! I can't fucking move my arms!"

"If this were a hit," I said, "You wouldn't be speaking or standing." Dave who sat quietly at the end of the table had a stunned look on his face. I stood up, walked around the table, and took Giacalone's pistol and knife from its holster and sheath.

"Relax. We're all friends here." Then pointing Giacalone's Colt.45 semiautomatic toward Vocarro, I said, "Isn't that right, Abe?"

"You're damn right **we** are!" Turning back to Giacalone, and pointing my finger at him, I said "sit!" Now able to move, Giacalone sat in his chair. Calmly, I walked back around the table with his weapons and reseated myself. Giacalone, now forced to be more amenable, blurted, "Friends, uh? Well, shit, I need a drink!"

"Later," I said and smiled.

"Whaddaya want from me, anyway?" Giacalone rasped.

"Something for your country."

"Country? HA! I don't work for my country."

"This is an exception."

"Oh yeah, how much is in it for me?" I stopped

smiling and looked directly at Giacalone's chest. The pain I inflicted with just my thoughts, lasted only long enough for him to clutch at his chest in a mix of terror and surprise. I made my point.

"How much is it worth to you, my friend, to breathe without permanent pain?"

Giacalone swallowed hard.

"It's worth whatever ya want me to do."

"Good. Now that's what I like to hear from my friends. I'm in the mood for making lots of friends today. In fact, some more of our country's helpers are on their way here now. The party starts once all our guests have arrived. Until then, hang tight, all will be clear soon enough." I called in another armed guard to keep a watch on Vocarro until it was time to greet the others. Dave and I escorted Giacalone out the door and had him wait just outside the library where we could still see him.

Dave trying hard to contain both confusion and awe about what he had just witnessed pulled me to the side and started talking in a hushed tone.

"Jeeze Bob, how in the hell did you do what you did in there?"

"Dave, what you saw in there is what I needed you to see. I don't have time to explain. And you wouldn't understand if I could." I could tell he still desperately wanted an explanation.

"Look, Dave, more will happen, and you will not understand the 'how' of it all. I need to know I can count on you. Can I count on you, Dave?"

"Okay, but I'm not sure I can handle any more surprises. That said, you can count on me Bob."

"Good, now I need you to hightail it to the airstrip and let me know as soon as our next guest arrives." He seemed relieved.

"We're good?" I gave him a friendly pat on the shoulder.

"Yeah, yeah, we're good." The Mafia killers were now an essential part of my assault teams, and with this alternate plan coming together I had to do my best to keep Vocarro's guys in my good graces. I turned my attention to Giacalone who was busy staking out the place and from the looks of it soon to lose his patience.

"Hungry?"

"Yeah. Where's the grub in this joint?"

"Follow me." I led him to the elegant, chandelier dining room and up to its long, fossil-stone dining table. The twenty-four members of Bernie's afternoon drill session gathered for a meal arranged by Frank. Every supply we needed, food, clothing or ammunition arrived via one of our Lear jets.

The decadent spread on the table was a magnificent culinary display-silver trays laden with succulent steaks and prime rib, chicken, lobster, shrimp and seafood, hors d'oeuvres, fruits, vegetables, cheese and pastries. It was a minor detail, but one that could provide the members with some sense of normalcy during what was for many of them a most unusual time.

When Giacalone entered the dining room, looking conspicuously out of place, the eyes of the members present recoiled in unison at the sight of him. I gestured to the trays of food.

"Help yourself and mind your manners." Giacalone nodded, then grunted.

I needed to have a word with Frank, who was at the other end of the room, and did not notice Giacalone heading toward Cheryl Lerner, a Fraternity member.

Cheryl, a strikingly beautiful, black woman in her mid-30s, dressed in loose-fitted hiking gear, was standing near the cheese dishes. Her training session with Bernie left her raven hair tousled, and she still had a touch of perspiration on her skin from the drills.

Giacalone apparently had an appetite for more than a meal.

"Ya work here, tits? This yer break?" Cheryl shot him a sharp look and turned away from him.

"The cold type, eh? Well, tits, make yerself useful. How 'bout movin' that nice ass and gettin' me a drink? What say a double Scotch, light on the ice. Looks like ya could use one too." He dug a finger into her ribs.

Cheryl instinctively slapped his finger away. Then, in a cultured and controlled voice full of venom, she faced him and looked into his eyes.

"I don't know who you think you are, but I suggest you get the hell away from me."

"Nah. I'm stayin' right here," he smirked lustily.

"Where's the help git off bein' so nasty, anyway?

Lucky fer you, I'm partial to black pussy. I'll show ya sweetie." With a lascivious grunt, Giacalone's right hand grabbed Cheryl's firm, round buttocks.

"Fleshy ass. Jest how I like it." Putting his arm around her shoulder, he slid his other hand downward towards her breasts.

"I know what ya cold ones… " Cheryl's swift elbow jabbed into his groin and he doubled over.

"Ya bitch, I'll… " The commotion caught my attention, and I instantly regretted taking my eyes off of Giacalone. I made my way over to the other side of the room and once again let my thoughts inflict pain. He let out an excruciating scream before his legs became soft and he collapsed writhing on the floor.

"I only jabbed him in the groin." Cheryl said. She seemed confused and shocked at how what she did could produce such an intense reaction. Giacalone's face was red and his body seemed contorted by involuntary spasms.

"Christ!" Frank yelled. "What the hell's going on?" Other members had gathered around. I berated myself for being careless. I hadn't prepared the members for the next phase of the plan.

"Goddamn, Bob!" Frank yelled.

"You can't let these Mafia people roam around freely like this." At the sound of the word mafia, all the members let out an audible gasp.

"Look, Cheryl, everybody, I'm sorry. This was all my fault. Forgive me. I'll explain later." I looked down at Giacalone, and with my thoughts relieved him of his pain then pulled him up to his feet. The man who only moments before was screaming in agony was now quiet and cooperative. I glimpsed at all the shocked faces. I had a hell of a lot of explaining to do. Frank was the first one to speak.

"Bob, what are you going to do about this?"

"You'll see, but for now I'm getting him out of here." I decided the gym was big enough to house my new friends. And given the invaluable lesson Giacalone just taught me, the paralysis trick would be vital to keeping all of them under control.

I just had to put my mind to it, as I'd done when I wanted access to their thoughts or needed to inflict pain. When I tried it on Giacalone, the terror in his eyes, the only part of his body still under his control, told me everything I needed to know. Paralysis scared the shit out of these mobsters.

By late evening, the rest of Vocarro's friends had arrived. I put a system in place. A greeting by me and Vocarro in the library and then off to join Giacalone and the others in the gym where they would remain in a state of paralysis. So much for getting them in my good graces.

I brought Dave and Frank to the gym so they could see for themselves I had the situation under control. The gym had plenty of space and included a shower-ing area, and an exercise facility, complete with weights, an inclined platform for situps, and a fixed pipe for isometric exercises.

Twenty-four mafia killers, plus Vocarro stood like

wax figures. In their wretched state, they could hear. They could breathe. They could smell. They could understand. But only their eyes could move, revealing the terror and anguish they felt. They were in speechless purgatory.

Dave stared as if he couldn't understand what he saw and yet he couldn't pull his attention away.

"Bob, how... how did you do this to them?"

"Don't ask Dave. I told you no questions. Just be thankful I can do it." Frank knew better than to ask questions. From there on, Dave referred to the Mafia killers in the gym as "those in cold storage."

CHAPTER 13

SUE WAS WORKING LATE, so I paid her a visit in the Bar Room. She was typing at her desk when she saw me.

"Bob!" she greeted me with one of her radiant smiles.

"What brings you in here?"

"Stopped by to let you know you can work in the library again, starting tomorrow." Just then I noticed how tired I was. The day's events were finally taking a toll on me.

Sue got up then and unexpectedly rushed over and embraced me.

"Thank you, darling, does this mean you have everything under control then?" While she held me, I could feel her heartbeat and instinctively and gently stepped back out of her embrace.

"Whoa there. Be careful how you address me Sue, especially on the job. People have enough to say around here." I could tell my words made her sad, and in that moment, I realized I didn't want to cause her sadness. I wanted more than anything to feel her embrace again.

"I'm sorry, Sue." I felt an overwhelming urge to touch her. Forgive me Gloria. Instead, I said, "You've had a long day. Why don't you take the rest of the evening off, relax? I'll see you back in our rooms."

"What will you be doing?"

"Not relaxing." I ran into Dave after leaving the Bar Room. He had just finished a call on his cloned phone.

"Bob, just received word the Sig-Sauer 928 pistols for our friends in cold storage were just flown in. Plenty of them, with silencers and box loads of 9mm ammunition, plus their gear."

"Good, now the real training can begin. First thing tomorrow assemble the members in the main room."

"You mean shit's about to hit the fan?"

"Yeah and guess who's going to have to help me clean up?" By the time I made it back to my room, I was weary with exhaustion. I asked myself for the hundredth time, why in hell did I ever accept this mission? And then I remembered.

As I was setting the alarm Sue opened the door connecting our rooms. Her reddish-gold hair glowing like a flame around her shoulders. She was wearing a white high scoop-jersey top, and dark chili crinkle linen shorts.

"You look exhausted," She said with a look of concern.

"Herding Vocarro and his boys wore me out. I need some rest." I stretched my shoulders as Sue came closer, then gently placed her fingers on my temples, and gently kneaded the tension away.

"You shouldn't have to handle them all on your

own." Her voice had taken on a protective tone. I held her eyes for a moment.

"Hell, I'm the only one who can do it."

"Still, you are only one man."

"I do what I have to, including what I must do tomorrow. The members won't like what I have to say." Sue kissed me gently on the forehead, and as she pulled back, a slight wisp of her hair fell over her eyes.

"Get some rest, Bob."

"You too."

Four hours later, my alarm went off, and I felt alert and ready for the day ahead. I dressed quickly and slowed down only when Sue, who was also up, caught my attention. The graceful way she carried herself was captivating.

"You will need nourishment for what is ahead of you," she smiled.

"Coffee and breakfast, darling? It's okay to call you darling in your room, isn't it?" The mere sight of her, and the sound of her voice, uplifted my spirits and brought a smile to my face.

"You're the darling," I said. "Bringing me breakfast like this."

"I will always be your darling," Sue said, the warmth in her eyes giving me the impression she meant it.

"I only wish the members I have to face this morning thought of me as a darling."

"You're the boss. They have to do what you say."

"Oh yeah, ever hear of mutiny?"

CHAPTER 14

ALL THE MEMBERS, dressed in their training gear for the morning session with Bernie, waited expectantly for me to begin.

"I know many of you have questions about what you witnessed in the dining room yesterday afternoon." I looked around at the anxious faces.

"Today, all will become clear, but before I continue, let me remind you all that you are honor-bound to carry out the plan, even if you do not agree with it." I gave them a moment to let that sink in.

"The man who caused the commotion yesterday, Roberto Giacalone is an associate of Abe Vocarro, a well-known mobster. He and other associates like him are here and will assist us with executing our attack on the Cyprus Group. I will pair each of you with one of Vocarro's associates on your mission." That was all it took to elicit loud vocalizations.

"Mobsters! No way we'll work with mafia killers!"

"Those savages could kill us!" a woman member cried out.

"Beat the Cyprus Group to the punch."

"Yeah!" others agreed from a din of heavy groans.

"I assure you, regardless of what you have

witnessed, the mobsters each of you will be paired with will be courteous and obedient."

Then the heckling erupted once again.

"Are you kidding?!" a male member snarled.

"That's bullshit!" another member shouted.

"And you know it!" I raised my hand and shouted with authority, "Calm down! Hear me out. You have my word that what you witnessed yesterday afternoon will not happen again." The shouts and groans slowly dissipated into silence.

"I'll prove it to you," I said calmly.

"Yeah... How?!" another skeptical voice challenged.

"Breakfast is waiting for you in the Bar Room, and I have canceled your morning training session. One hour from now I will deliver the proof you want." One member stared at me bleakly, and warned, "This better not be one of your sleight-of-hand tricks."

"You be the judge," I smiled. My sleight of hand was my ace in the hole.

"Show time!" I said to Bernie and Clyde, taking them with me to the gym.

"We have one hour so let's move," I said. As instructed, Frank and Dave got to work setting up a sturdy table and comfortable chairs on one side of the gym. I wanted the mobsters well-fed in the hopes this would help increase the odds the next phase of my plan would go as smoothly as possible. Offering them a sumptuous spread and non-alcoholic beverages was an excellent place to start.

Vocarro and twenty-four of his associates stood

before me in a state of paralysis, most with their lids half-lowered. They ranged in age from late 20s to mid-fifties, were mostly husky, and had shoulder meat and necks as broad as their jaw, though a few were lean. Some wore impeccably tailored suits, others loose-fitted shabby outfits. A few were hulking men, downright ugly, who would give Quasimodo a run for his money.

It was time to prepare them to meet the members. I stood in front of each one.

"I will release you from your paralyzed state. When I do, you will remember nothing that has previously happened to you at this villa, and if you never want this paralysis to overtake you again, you will obey what I, the Red Baron, wants you to do at all times. Do you agree to this?"

Without exception, each killer vigorously blinked his eyes, showing agreement.

"Remember, if you break this agreement, you will automatically return to this paralyzed state. Now, when I release you, you will remain still, listen quietly and carefully to what I want you to do."

More blinking of eyes. When all the men stood quietly, I motioned for one guard to join me.

"You will go to the showering area, clean up quickly, shave, then put on these clothes and return here. And be quick about it."

Once they were all showered and changed. I addressed the group again and began by gesturing to the table.

"I want you to walk to that table, slowly, sit in the nearest empty chair, eat, drink and mind your manners. No noisy or disruptive behavior. When a group of people enter, I will tell you to stop eating and drinking. You will rise and greet these people politely and treat them with kindness and respect. Do you understand all I have asked you to do?" Reverently, solemnly, each killer either nodded, or said, "Yes" or "yeah." There was one grunt signaling the same.

I watched in relief and amazement as they all carried out my instructions. Many speaking with a Sicilian dialect, a lot of "dese" and "dose" and "dems" thrown in. Some voices were monotonic. Others raspy. Some spoke in flat tones; others with more timbre and inflections. Some were soft-spoken. Entirely absent were any mean stares or the noisy, deep-throated bravado and ebullient braggadocio characteristic of them before.

I was pleased.

After about ten minutes of watching their tactful indulgences, I signaled to Dave, and he left the gym. When the twenty-four Fraternity members were outside the gym entrance, I addressed the mobsters.

"Eating, drinking and talking time is over." Immediately, everyone at the table desisted with their activities and instantly rose to their feet, standing still, with friendly smiles on their faces. I watched the Fraternity members make their way inside. All eyes were on the mobsters. The expressions on the members' faces were a mix of fear, shock and relief.

"Ladies and gentlemen," I began and waved my right hand toward the table, "Meet the Cyd Group!"

"These are killers?!" one female member muttered.

"Yes," I smiled. "All friendly fellows to you."

"You have these guys on dope or something?" a male member said, his voice skeptical.

"Just my charm, which they will obey, without fail. But they're charming all on their own."

"Shit! They are," another member called out.

"Look, why not see for yourselves? Mingle with them. Talk about anything. They're excited to meet you." After some hesitation, yet unable to resist their curiosity, a few of the members ventured to mingle with some of the killers. Those who needed more time looked on. Within a few minutes, casual chatting turned into friendly conversation, even an occasional outbreak of laughter, putting at ease the remainder of the members, who then joined in with the mingling leading to smiles of acceptance.

I nodded to Frank, who brought forth a small straw basket and set it on the table.

"Please, may I have everyone's attention? In this basket are all the names of Vocarro's associates, each of their names typed on a separate slip of paper. Each fraternity member will draw one slip from the basket, and the name appearing on that slip will be your assault team partner. Let's begin!"

The mood had lifted, and all members were much more receptive to the plan now that I followed through on giving them the proof they needed.

Cheryl Lerner, the last one to draw from the basket, seemed visibly upset by the name on her slip of paper.

"Him?!" The name on the slip was Roberto Giacalone.

"Bob, I can't!" she yelled out. I raised a hand, motioning for her to stop and listen.

"Cheryl, hear me out." Then addressing all the members, I said, "If anyone has reservations about the partner I have assigned, take me at my word when I tell you, your partner will be under your complete control at all times." Cheryl did not look reassured by my words.

"Everyone, pair up with your partners and wait for me to come to you." I then formally introduced each of Vocarro's associates to their assigned Fraternity member partners.

I began with Cheryl and Giacalone.

"Giacalone, this is Cheryl Lerner, she's your boss acting on my authority. From here on in you will protect your boss and do exactly what your boss tells you to do, without hesitation, without question, and with the utmost of respect."

All the Mafia killers knew what would happen to them if they didn't obey the Red Baron's command. I allowed all the members and their partner associates another hour to become better acquainted.

Cheryl Lerner still seemed unconvinced. She put Giacalone to the test. She approached Giacalone with an alluring smile, and said, "Let's take a walk."

"Yes, ma'am," Giacalone said. "Anywhere you want."

As the two casually walked toward a door exiting the gym, Cheryl made it a point to flirt with him as she pushed her black hair in a gleaming spill over her shoulders.

But Giacalone had no response to her feline grace. It was as if he hadn't even noticed. Once they were outside standing on a grassy knoll with a view of the lake, Cheryl began.

"Have you ever seen me before today?"

"No, ma'am."

"Are you certain of that? We didn't meet in the dining room yesterday?"

"You must be confusin' me with some other dude, Miss Lerner. I never saw you before today. Nowhere."

"What do you think I do?" Cheryl asked innocently as they strolled along the grass, her steps less graceful, her stride stretching her slacks across her thighs in a deliberate sway of her behind, fine and lithe.

"Yer my boss, and a friend of the Red Baron. That's all that matters to me," he said with a tone of indifference. But undaunted, her course set in what she wanted to achieve, the beautiful features of Chery's face seemed to loosen, as did the dignity of her cultured voice, and feigning a seductive smile, she abruptly asked,

"You like my tits? Nice ones, right?" Giacalone expression tightened.

"It's not my place to notice," he said guardedly.

"Aw, come on, Roberto," Cheryl taunted him with a salacious wink.

"We're alone now." As she spoke, she twisted the tight curve of her derriere, then added, "I think you are just dying to grab my ass!"

"That don't make no sense, ma'am." But Cheryl pressed on, determined, spurred by her quest.

"Sense or not," she said, her voice softening, "it is your kind of fleshy ass. R-E-A-L fleshy!" Her voice now was almost an alluring whisper, one she thought had to be irresistible to him.

"And it is just waiting for your fingers. So, come'on."

Giacalone's jaw muscles rippled. He looked appalled rather than aroused, and hesitant.

"That a command, Miss Lerner?" he asked.

"No. No command. But how can you resist?" she sighed.

"Cause that won't be protectin' ya, ma'am, like the Red Baron sez." In that moment, Cheryl's total affectation faded, her uncertainties about Giacalone fading with it.

"You are correct, Roberto," she said, dignity returning her scholarly demeanor. "And since we will work together, even though I am your boss, please address me as Cheryl, not ma'am nor Miss Lerner. "Okay?"

"Okay," Giacalone sighed. "I do what you want, Cheryl." With the meet-and-greet over and the assault teams successfully paired I could now turn my attention to forming the air groups.

I had Dave take the Cyd Group to their new accommodations, which would include regular mealtimes, a comfortable bed, access to bathroom facilities and more freedom to move under the watchful eyes of our guards.

Vocarro's associates whom I tagged as the "Cyd group" were under my control and the control of Fraternity members. But unlike with the mobsters, I couldn't control the Fraternity members with my thoughts. I had to outsmart them when possible.

CHAPTER 15

THE FIRST ORDER OF BUSINESS concerning the air groups was meeting with Dave, my point man who I most relied on to ensure Fraternity members carried out their duties as planned. Dave would also ensure our fleet of jets were ready, and our pilots trained to carry out the attack. In the afternoon, he made sure all twenty-four members of the air groups, except for Kym, assembled in the living room.

The Fraternity members chosen for the air groups were not in the best physical shape and lacked the stamina needed to engage in the rigorous training the assault groups required.

"I know many of you are wondering what role you will play in Friday's attack against the Cyprus Group. I will share that with you in a moment, but before I do, I would like to remind you I expect you to carry out my orders as you have all agreed to do. The Fraternity's survival depends on your contribution." I paused for a moment.

"Many of you have seen the assault teams assemble for training. Your contribution will be to serve as members of our air group."

"What the hell are air groups?"

"Air groups deliver the assault teams by jet to their

targets." Many of the members let out an audible gasp.

"That... that's damn dangerous! We're not trained for that. Bob, what exactly are you expecting us to do?"

"On Thursday, the day before the attack, you will carry out a reconnaissance flight over the target area and using specialized cameras will take pictures of potential obstacles the assault teams need to know about. On Friday, the day of the attack, you will deliver your assigned assault team to the targets."

"Hold on! Are you saying that we deliver both the assault teams to their targets on Friday and do a reconnaissance of the target the day before, on Thursday?"

"You got it," I answered. "You will begin training on mock reconnaissance flights tomorrow."

"Oh, hell!"

"I can't do all of that."

"You'll do it. That's an order!" That brought on groans of anxiety and disbelief. Convincing this group to do their part would be much more difficult than I had hoped.

"Each air group is assigned a specific assault team. The air group's first task is to see that the pilot lands on the predetermined landing strip reconnoitered the day before. There, a car will be waiting. While the armed Fraternity member of the air group remains behind with the pilot — protecting him from a surprise attack and making sure he doesn't scram before the assault team's return. The assault team and the air group's armed guard member leave the aircraft and enter the waiting car. The guard member then drives the assault team to the targeted Cyprus Group location."

As I spoke, groans of opposition and despair spread across the room.

"The guard," I continued, "waits in the parked car, while the assault team enters the residence and accomplishes their mission. Once the assault team gets back to the car, the guard hauls-ass back to the jet, and the pilot flies everyone back to the villa."

"Questions?" From the shocked faces, one male member had the spunk to break free from the melody of moans, and said, "Yeah... I have a question. What do we do if after delivering the assault team something unforeseen happens to it? Like if it gets wiped out or they do not kill the targeted people?" Without a moment's hesitation, I responded.

"Then that job goes to you. The air group becomes the assault team, your guard teammate becomes the killer under your direction." An uproar of "what?!" spread across the members.

"Quiet!" I raised my hand "Everyone calm down! We must kill Cyprus Group members! No matter the cost, else we're all dead," I reminded them.

"The unexpected will happen, and when it sticks up its ugly head, we must meet it with resilience and do what is necessary to save the Fraternity."

"They will slaughter us!" someone yelled.

"Not if you heed your training, so enough whining

and pay attention! Your prime focus is your reconnaissance flight on Thursday. After that preparation for the assault flights on Friday. There will be more on the specifics of Friday later, as your training progresses. But for now, I want to go over the important aspects of the two mock reconnaissance flights each of you will be flying. The first tomorrow, on Tuesday, and the second on Wednesday. On these flights, your pilots will be your best friends, for they will be thoroughly instructed on how to train you. It is vital that you watch and learn from your pilot, what he is doing... how he is handling the aircraft in filming objects below with the jet's camera... asking him pertinent questions related to effective reconnaissance. All of this to know exactly what to do and what to expect when it is for real on Thursday." I complemented these instructions with the showing of a video on air reconnaissance, discussing it as we went along, and answering questions. In between I had to endure an outcry of griping, the main gripe relating back to an air group having to become an assault team.

"If you become an assault team, watching tomorrow morning's assault team training sessions will prepare you. Dave will make sure you're all there." In hearing one last wave of audible opposition I concluded the meeting.

CHAPTER 16

THE DISGRUNTLED SESSION with the newly assigned air team members left me ragged. There were still crucial matters left unresolved. And too little time to address them. Do we... I... have enough time? I kept asking myself.

Sue was waiting up for me when I got to my room. She looked concern the moment she saw me.

"Darling, you look like hell!"

"That's an ingratiating thing to say to your tired boss." Sue moved gracefully toward me and placed two consoling fingers on my chin.

"An overworked boss," she said before bringing her supple body up against mine, the light scent of a delicate perfume titillating my senses. She kissed me gently on the cheek, then began kneading her fingers through my mussed hair, and massaging my scalp.

"You need to relax." This definitely was not part of her secretarial duties, but I wasn't about to complain. It made up for my entire day.

"I know you hardly eat when you work, so I had dinner brought up for you, filet mignon and potatoes to go with a Paul Mason California Red. Does that earn me a kiss, boss?" I didn't know the etiquette for this, nor at the moment did I care. I was hungry. Gratefully, I gave her a peck on the lips. I intended for it to be light, but her full, moist lips sucked me in, so warm; so yielding, and her breath so sweet, I momentarily forgot about dinner. When we finally pulled away from one another Sue was the first to speak.

"Thank you," she said in a voice so soft it was almost a whisper.

"No, thank you Sue," I said, still reeling from the unexpected moment exchange between us. We sat at a small table in my room. Sue watched as I savored every bite, even as my eyelids grew heavy for sleep.

"I heard you stopped the mutiny," she said.

"You can say that, but it took a toll on me."

"After dinner, promise you'll go straight to bed."

During the next two days, Tuesday and Wednesday, the pressure of time was mounting. The air groups still harboring powerful doubts and fears about the mission made for a challenge I could do without. Meanwhile, training the assault teams and their Cyd Group counterparts was also about to begin.

Outside the villa was an Olympic size swimming pool surrounded with lounge chairs and small tables. Facing one end of the pool was a large pale pink pavilion in the shape of a half-shell overlooking a marble floor. The pavilion was large enough for assault team training sessions with Fraternity members and their Cyd Group partners.

In attendance to observe the training were all the

prospective members of the air groups and their previously selected teammate guards.

I paced back-and-forth in front of forty-eight expectant faces. They all conceptually understood their role in Friday's attack, but now with their team training about to begin, the reality of what they must do would hit home. I needed to prepare them mentally, not just physically.

"The first thing you need to know," I began my pre-training address to those gathered, "is who's in charge. The boss of each assault team is its Fraternity member. Fraternity members will handle door locks, security alarms, and will know about potential obstacles reported by air group reconnaissance. Cyprus Group member targets will be at their residence at the designated time. Once your jet lands, an air group guard will drive you to a location that is close enough to the target residence so you may advance on foot." I paused, pushing my hands out if front of me for emphasis.

"Every assault team will have a map marking the car parking location and the assault location, along with photos of the intended target or targets, gloves, a Sig Sauer pistol with a GSG 1911 .22LR Silencer and black masks which you will put on once you reach the residence. Speed and surprise are the keys to your success. Once you're on the property, you must eliminate all occupants including security you may encounter. When you've completed your mission, your job is to get back to the parked vehicle as quickly as possible." A Fraternity member raised his hand.

"Bob, what if things don't go as smoothly as you just laid them out?"

"You must rely on your training, improvise when needed and respond quickly and decisively to whatever comes your way."

Another question.

"What if there are children inside, or others aside from security people who are not Cyprus Group members? Do we kill them too?"

"I assure you, you will find no children inside, nor any other adults who are not Cyprus Group members, except for security people. Kill everyone inside the residence. You get in and out quickly." Then a more frantic question that brought on a hush of silence.

"What if we're killed first?"

"Your training will prevent that from happening. But I urge you not to dwell on that possibility."

"Other questions?" There were none.

"Let's get on with the training." Since Clyde was the only guard with combat military experience, I selected him to train the assault teams.

Clyde used dummies to simulate the techniques most efficient for killing success and reducing the odds of personal harm. All members of the assault teams had their turn while air group members watched uneasily from the sidelines.

"Speed, speed, speed!" Clyde kept repeating as he repeated the movements for the others to model. "Don't give dem an opportunity to react." As the training continued, they placed the dummies in various discovery positions, including lying in bed or dealing with security personnel so myriad attacks could be simulated. Each assault team had thirteen SIG FMJ Center fire Pistol Cartridges in the magazine. The drills continued for several hours.

At the end of the training session, I walked with Clyde out of the pavilion.

"Well, Clyde, what do you think? How are they coming along?"

"The killers on yer teams have that killer instinct but can't say the same about yer Fraternity members. Could cause hesitation… the difference between life and death in a critical moment." Shaking his head, Clyde reluctantly added, "Boss, dey could screw up your operation before their Cyd Group partners have time to do any killin.'"

"Look, I know I'm asking a lot, but you think you can work on instilling the killer instinct in them in tomorrow's practice assaults?"

Clyde spit on the ground then with a face dripping with sweat he looked at me before answering.

"I'll try, boss, but yer Fraternity buddies are awful amateurs."

"Just give it your best shot!"

The conversation with Clyde left me uneasy. I can't have the Fraternity members screw this up. They're all I've got. And what if Fraternity members got killed? The repercussions would be dire, but at that moment another more chilling preoccupation entered my mind, Sue!

Sue was one of the few people unarmed and unprepared to deal with a Cyprus attack. I hastened to catch up with Clyde again.

"Clyde, I need you to go to my office, get Sue and take her to the firing range. Show her how to use the pistol and prepare for an attack. Tell her it's on my orders. And Clyde, I need you to do it now!"

"Yeah sure, boss," Clyde said though he seemed taken aback by the sudden request.

"And one more thing, make sure she's back at the shooting range for more training in the morning before you train the assault teams."

That off my mind, I set off to find Bernie so he could get the guards on double alert for anything suspicious on the property, and Dave to assemble the assault team members.

"Bob, can it wait! That was one hell of a training session this morning."

"Do it now, Dave!"

I waited for the Fraternity members to assemble in the main living room. I didn't care how tired they were, this was a critical window of opportunity to talk some sense into them and I had to take it.

"What the hell's wrong with you people? Your performance this morning, is not going to cut it!" That elicited a barrage of tired moans.

"The hell with your moans," I continued.

"Your lack of demonstrating a killer instinct leaves

you indecisive in making accurate decisions under stress, which renders you vulnerable to potential screw ups and open to jeopardizing this entire operation. Not to mention your lives!" I paused, stared back at the members for emphasis.

"I will have none of this! I will tolerate no screw-ups! To ensure there are none, Cyd Group members will now be in charge." That fostered a mood of panic.

"Don't you dare make those degenerates bosses over us!" Cheryl Lerner yelled out.

"No!... No!... No!" the members chanted in unison.

"Then you damn well get your asses in gear and show me that decision isn't necessary," I yelled back.

"Show me you have what it takes. Show it to Clyde in your stimulated training performances tomorrow."

"Are you with me on this?"

"Yes!" came a resounding, unanimous roar. I noted the look of readiness in their eyes and it was all I needed to see. Once the assault team members cleared the room Dave brought in the air groups. Questions rang out almost immediately.

"Are you going to put us through all that killing stuff the assault teams had to suffer through with Clyde today?"

"Only If I feel the assault teams cannot do their jobs so you better damn well pay attention, because if that happens you're up."

"Christ!"

"For now, your focus should be on the first mock reconnaissance flight you will make today, in under an hour. Dave has made all the arrangements. Just remember everything we discussed yesterday. Until this is over, you can forget your martinis and focus on what's up ahead."

Most of the members stared at me as if they could use a double martini, straight.

I ended the session with a rejuvenating pitch similar in spirit to the one I had given earlier to members of the assault teams, then I turned them over to Dave.

Before calling it a day, I paid a visit to the Cyd Group in the gym. As far as the killer instinct was concerned, thank the Gods these guys had it.

Sue was waiting up for me when I got to my room. She looked as lovely as ever in her white scoop neck dress, sitting on the edge of my bed and looking down at the Sig-Sauer 928 she was holding in her hand.

"Darling, what is going on? Why did you order Clyde to teach me how to use and fire this weapon? Are we under some kind of threat the guards can't handle?" Her eyes hinted at alarm, even though her voice was matter of fact.

I stood there for a few moments staring at her, letting her words register, and considering how best to respond. Finally, with little energy, I said, "It's a precautionary measure, in case the Cyprus Group gets wind of what we're up to and attacks us first. If such an event happens, I want everyone armed and able to protect themselves."

"Is that likely? This location is difficult to find."

"I'm taking no chances, especially not with you. Better be prudent now than sorry later." At this, her demeanor seemed to brighten.

"Then it isn't likely," she exclaimed with relief.

"Oh, my poor darling, you're letting everything get to you."

"Probably so, I uttered quietly."

"But thank you for wanting to protect me... caring about me," she said, her voice and eyes now softer.

"And to show you how much I care for you... to ease your mind about what the outside world might do to me, I'll attend to my training without complaint." My tired eyes blinked a look of tenderness at her.

"I wish I didn't have to put you through this." Sue's eyes flashed back tenderness in return.

"You warned me Bob, and I accepted. Still, I think you're being overly cautious. It's not what I'm going through. It's what you're going through. It's just too much!" Then laying aside the pistol, patting the blanket on the bed, she softly motioned for me to join her.

"Come, sit down beside me. You look like you can barely stand up."

I eased down beside her, and released a lengthy sigh, "Damn world. Full of never-ending futility. Is it worth fighting over? Christ, what the hell are we doing?"

"Now stop that! You're exhausted, that's all." She stroked my face, then kissed me lightly on the lips.

"You need your sleep. Let's call it a night."

CHAPTER 17

EARLY WEDNESDAY MORNING, Sue and I rushed through coffee and breakfast. Her morning training session with Clyde would begin shortly. Before leaving, instead of the usual peck on the lips, Sue gave me a deeper kiss. A kiss of yearning and passion. It touched my soul and left me with a sense of unease. I was not ready for the amorous feelings the kiss seemed to awaken within me.

"Bye for now, darling. Hope to see you later." When I was alone again, I silently berated myself for what I was feeling, a strange stillness, but there was no time to contemplate this stillness, except to mumble to myself,

"Forgive me, Gloria."

In the Bar Room, Frank and Dave were talking amongst themselves, waiting for me to begin our morning conference.

"How did the air group do on its mock flight yesterday?" was the first question I put to Dave as I took my seat at the conference table. Dave gave a slight shrug before answering.

"Rough going, Bob. But I'll see to it they perform better and will get them ready to deliver the intel we need on Thursday."

"Frank, how are you coming along on the rest?"

"After the feedback I got from you and Dave, I put together the flight manifests, a schedule for staggered departures based on time zones, and a list of all the refueling sites. We still need to decide on the assault team and air group pairings."

"Good. What about the attack itself? Have you worked out the time?" I asked.

"As you requested, Bob. Same local time in every time zone." We were making headway on our plan and strategy, but I couldn't shake the nagging thought that even the best-laid plan can fall to disaster at a moment's notice. If we didn't pull this off, I wouldn't get to see and speak to Gloria's spirit, a potential consequence I could not bear. I asked Frank to go into specific detail about the plans, and by the time we'd gone over everything; it was lunchtime. Bernie brought in ham sandwiches, coffee and pastries.

"Well, Bob, what do you think?" Frank asked.

"Commendable work, both of you." I said. Frank was rubbing his lower lip, and I could tell something was on his mind.

"Bob, with all due respect, I hope this plan comes off like clockwork."

I took a moment before responding.

"Things never come off like clockwork, Frank. Let's make sure this plan is tight as possible." I paused.

"I think we're done here. Dave, assemble the air groups, let's give 'em their flight schedules." I left the Bar Room thinking about Frank's words. I felt certain about one thing. We could plan, and we could train, but there is no way to predict a flawless execution. Attempting to do so would be futile.

As expected, the air group members were still on edge about their role in the Cyprus Group attack. I could see the anxiety in their tired faces, the way their eyes averted from mine when I made eye contact. They're not ready and we're running out of time, I thought.

"Today, you will receive your flight manifestos and departure schedules. It is imperative that we keep to the plan. Later flight departures will depend on earlier flights returning on time." In response to this, Jethro Wolff, the oldest of the Fraternity members, spoke up.

"My God, Bob, we'll be flying on little more than a wing and a prayer. On crossed fingers that good fortune will spare our asses."

"Do I need to remind you, you agreed to carry out your part in all this?" I paused, knowing I had to shake him and the rest of this group up.

"Jeth, spare me your eloquence on asses and stop wasting valuable time with complaints. Man-up!" I turned away from Jeth's red face to the rest of the group.

"All of you, concentrate on your reconnaissance training flight today. That's when you will pick up something that might spare your fellow members' asses."

After the mock reconnaissance flights had taken off, I caught up with Clyde. He was out by the combat training area.

"Well, Clyde, compared to yesterday, how did they do this morning?"

"Boss, ya kicked some ass, dey had mor life in 'em this morning." Clyde seemed pleased to report, but I noted a look of concern.

"You have something else you want to tell me?"

Clyde hesitated. "That gal of yers, boss, Sue. She definitely has the killer instinct."

"What do you mean?"

"She's something else with that pistol, boss," Clyde looked perplexed.

"Makin' quick decisions with it, the right ones, like a pro. I got a touch about dese things. Sue is more than ya think she is."

"What the hell are you suggesting?" Clyde hesitated again, giving me a hard, troubled look,

"Jest that somethin' is odd here, boss. Somethin' fishy about her. Not bein' a member or guard, how easy she puts up with our goings-on, not bothered by 'em, pickin' up on our plans. Reminds me of my time in Iraq. We had someone in our ranks jest like Sue, who turned out to be a spy."

I froze. Sue, a Cyprus Group spy? Could it be true? My God! I had to find out.

"Clyde, don't tell anyone else about this unless I tell you to."

"Gotcha, boss."

I went to the office in the library where Sue, Dave and Bernie were working. Dave and Sue were going over scheduling notes at her desk.

"Bob, dar..." Sue caught herself.

"Everyone relax!" I said, with a note of forced cheer in my voice.

"Sue, your training with Clyde is over."

"Did I scare him off?" she smiled.

"Not at all, in fact, he's impressed by your skill, said not much more he can teach you."

"He is great at what he does." Sue said. Deciding on a bold move in the presence of Dave and Bernie, I had to address Clyde's concerns.

"Sue, I'd like you to join me tonight for a special dinner in your honor."

"A special dinner? For me?" She said, her face beaming.

"You've earned it! Wear something nice." I hated to do it, but I needed to put Sue off guard, in the hopes she would let something slip if in fact she was a Cyprus Group plant.

"Bernie, you arrange for dinner at my room this evening, and Dave, make sure it's delicious. We owe Sue exactly what she's given us, the very best."

That evening, I drew open the terrace drapes in my room to reveal a darkening night sky. I put on a tailored blue suit, crisp white shirt and a red tie.

Bernie and two other guards brought in a small, rosewood pedestal dining table, matching rosewood chairs with cushioned backs, and Cabriole legs. They set the table with silverware, crystal, and candles. Soft, ambient music filled the room. The last touch was a dimming of the lights to create the atmosphere I wanted.

When Sue entered the room, she was wearing a gem-trimmed buttercup tank-top and a colorful, soft chiffon wrap skirt.

I motioned for Sue to sit at the table and pulled out her chair.

"I hope all this meets your satisfaction, Sue." I said as I gestured to the surrounding space and looked at her. She was a vision of loveliness, and her scent was intoxicating. Everything about her was. The sensuous gleam in her eyes as she looked at me with both longing and admiration.

"It's magical, darling. Everything is beautiful. You are beautiful. Thank you for all this." She took a sip of her aperitif and I gulped mine down.

They set a sumptuous dinner before us, lamb, chilled asparagus with mayonnaise, rice pilaf, soft cheeses, fresh baked bread, fruit, and a bottle of Chateau Latour, 1985.

"Enjoy, boss, and you too, Miss Bishop," Bernie grinned at us before leaving.

"Dining by candlelight is so romantic, darling. I can't thank you enough for this lovely evening." I had just opened the wine and was pouring a glass for each of us when Sue smiled and said in a soft, dream-like tone.

"I feel I'm on my honeymoon."

"Now don't get carried away."

"You don't like me being romantic?" Sue asked coyly, while pushing out her lips in a tantalizing pout.

"How about we limit romance to just one toast?" I said and lifted my wineglass.

"To you, darling." Sue said. She's doing one hell of a job keeping me off stride, I mused. With this in mind, for my toast, I said, "May I be able to match your kindness, Sue." For a moment, I felt a twinge of sadness at the mere thought my careful plans could be derailed by the beautiful creature sitting across from me.

"Have you ever been in military service? Police work? Anything like that?" My question took her by surprise.

"Heavens no! I would have told you. Why do you ask?"

"Just my form of pillow talk." I said, and she laughed.

"Darling, I'm afraid you could use some lessons in pillow talk."

Once we ate our fill and finished the wine, I poured us both some cognac, held up my glass and touched it gently to hers.

"Your turn to make the first toast," she said.

"Here's to the Cyprus Group," I took a sip and watched Sue's expression.

"Bob! I'm worried about you."

"And I'm worried about you," I said.

She got up from the table and moved over to the bed where she sat to remove her sandals. As she moved, I glimpsed a bare thigh and wondered if this was all part of her ruse. I got up and sat on the edge of the bed next to her. She leaned her body against mine before looking up at me with longing.

"Can I sleep with you tonight, boss?" Her voice was breathy, perhaps an aftereffect from the wine, or else it was all part of her plan. Seduction was a useful tool, I'd give her that.

"That's not included with the dinner," I said.

"Then let's make it part of dinner," she whispered, then softly licked my ear. Her sexuality and blatant expression of desire was almost too much. I had to stay in control. If I don't act now, I'm a goner, I thought.

Breaking free of her powerful wiles before I succumbed to them, I leapt up from the bed.

"We can't make love. Not tonight!"

"No? Then when? Tomorrow night?"

"Okay, tomorrow night."

"Is that a promise?" I would say anything to keep her from sweeping me into her bag. I didn't dare risk not being able to kill off the Cyprus Group and lose out on seeing Gloria's spirit because of a fling. And besides that, if Sue was a Cyprus Group spy, I couldn't well let her live.

"That's a promise," I said.

"You're such a darling," she purred, then caressed my cheek.

"So are you. Why don't you head to your room? Big day tomorrow I need some sleep."

On Thursday morning, Sue, in her usual cheerful disposition, brought breakfast into my room. Not having the absolute certainty she was a spy, meant I had to put in extra effort to keep our interactions as close to normal as she would expect them to be.

"Coffee, darling?"

"No, thank you, my lovely. I'd better be off." I said and made for the door.

"Everything will be fine," she called out, her smile at first reassuring and then mischievous. "Don't forget about tonight. You promised."

"I won't." I said before leaving the room. Either that or you'll be dead I mused.

Dave, driving the Fraternity Mercedes, was returning to the villa. He'd just sent off the first air group on their reconnaissance flight. As soon as he parked, I hopped into the passenger seat.

"Christ, Bob," Dave grimaced, "You look like Hell!"

"There's something urgent we need to deal with."

"What is it?!"

"Since we arrived here, have you observed anything odd regarding Sue's behavior? Any unusual cloned phone calls, questionable messages or notes? Anything at all that caught your attention?"

"Well, no. I would have reported anything unusual to you. As far as I can tell Sue has diligently carried out the duties you prescribed for her, and our inter-action has been pleasant except for when Vocarro's associates arrived, but under those circumstances that seemed a normal enough response."

Maybe she hadn't made her move yet. Perhaps she was waiting until the right moment to pass on infor-mation and derail our plans.

"Bob, the only thing I find strange is you question-ing me about Sue. Has she done anything we should worry about?"

"Maybe. Probably," I said painfully. "War has its spies."

"Sue, a spy?"

"I have reason to suspect it, Dave."

"Sue? Sweet Sue?" Dave clutched the steering wheel hard. He was taking the news a lot harder than I expected.

"Damn it, Dave, don't go freaking out on me. I need your help! We need to figure out if she is or isn't a spy and fast. We have too little time." Dave eased his grip on the wheel and turned to me.

"Help? What help, Bob? Jesus!"

"Calm yourself and listen." First, forget about attending to the second and third air groups when they're about to leave. I'll have Bernie attend to that. He knows what to do. Sue will be in the library soon. I want you to be her new best friend. I need your eyes and ears on everything she says and does, including phone calls she makes, and notes she writes. Everything! And then I need you to report back to me."

"You want me to spy on Sue?"

"If you care about saving our asses, don't let her out of your sight."

"What if she goes into the bathroom?" Dave asked in a tone that showed how uneasy he was about this whole arrangement.

"I sure as hell can't follow her in there."

"Install one of our portable audio-video units in the bathroom."

"Bob! Are you sure that's necessary?"

"Do it! And when Sue goes on her lunch break, use your charm and offer to accompany her."

"I'm not that much of a charmer, Bob."

"I'm sure Kym would disagree. One other thing. Have someone go to Sue's room and inspect it for anything suspicious. And make sure they leave no evidence of their inspection."

"Got all that, Dave?"

"Yes, yes, but Jesus!"

"In one hour I want a report on that room."

"Bob, what if she is a spy?" I didn't answer.

"You can't seriously be thinking what I think you're thinking?!"

"Just do what I've asked! You think this is any less devastating for me? I'm the one who has to make the decision."

CHAPTER 18

AS TROUBLING AS THE POSSIBILITY of Sue being a spy was, I had to push the matter out of my mind long enough to focus on the progress we were making with the air groups.

The Bar Room, where Frank, Clyde and two air group guards sat huddled together to review the aerial footage from the day's reconnaissance flights held a tense atmosphere. Through the haze of cigarette smoke I could make out from the countless empty coffee mugs and full ashtrays that everyone's nerves were on edge.

"How's the footage so far Frank?" I asked.

"Helpful, off to a good start."

"Good, we'll need as much intel as possible. Frank, Clyde, let's make sure we got a handle on security personnel, residence entry points, and any on-site security our Fraternity assault teams may encounter."

"On it! Have a look at some footage, Bob." A beautiful single-family home with enormous windows, a wrap-around terrace and two-car garage sitting on half an acre of land came into view. Just one block away there was a harbor about 3 miles long. Another residence popped up on the screen, larger than the first one. We'd have to adjust our approach based on the property size if we could ever hope to pull off our attack as quickly as possible.

"Clyde, I need you to work with Frank on altering the timeline where necessary. We don't have time to lose so let's make sure we've got a plan based on property size and location. We need our people in and out."

Clyde's military experience was critical to the mission's success but the thought of having to change our tactics brought on an uneasy feeling. And yet, there was an unexpected benefit to making changes in our plan. If Sue was indeed a spy, and we kept her in the dark about our altered attack strategy, she would be unable to act against our operation, especially during the critical final hours.

"You got it boss!" Clyde said, not looking nearly as on edge as the rest of us.

Two hours into our review of the aerial footage we had a crapload of alterations to make to our plan. Wealthy Cyprus Group members meant they had enough money to own land, and big homes, which translated into more planning for assault team drop offs and accurate estimates for making it through residence entry points. The tension in the Bar Room had increased significantly since I had arrived when Bernie unexpectedly burst into the room.

"Boss, Dave asked that I deliver this to you right away!" He handed me a folded slip of paper, which I opened without a moment's hesitation.

Search of room negative.
Observations thus far, not suspicious.
—Dave

I refolded the note and stuck it into my pocket. If Sue is a spy, she's damned good I mused.

"Thanks Bernie." Frank who had stopped watching the footage waited for Bernie to leave before saying anything.

"Must be something important."

"You, me and Clyde need to talk, privately." Frank gave the guards a short nod and gestured toward the door. I watched them leave and took a moment to collect my thoughts.

"Frank, how did you come to recommend Sue to me as my personal secretary?"

"Expert Search, their specialty is finding qualified people quickly. They sent me Sue's credentials in business and secretarial services, and she was available to begin immediately."

"Other than what the search firm sent you was there any more vetting done?"

"No, I mean the firm has a solid reputation, I relied on them to do the vetting for us?"

"I think it's possible you, I, this whole operation was tricked."

"Bob, what are you talking about?"

"I'm talking about the possibility that Expert Search is aligned with the Cyprus Group, and that Sue has been planted to spy on us." I watched Frank's face carefully as he considered my accusation.

"Have you gone mad again?!"

"I wish I was Frank. Clyde, tell him exactly what you told me yesterday about Sue. Everything!" Clyde snapped to attention and began.

"Sue is more dan you think. Way she holds the gun. Shoots and don't miss a target. Make no sense how a secretary could do that. In combat situations like deese, I'm never wrong. She's gotta be a spy."

"Sue a spy! Our entire mission in jeopardy! How? How sure are we?"

"Look Frank, I won't do anything about her until I have certainty. You and Clyde keep quiet about this until I do. So far, I don't think she's made a move against us, else today's reconnaissance flights would have met with some trouble."

"Are you going to have her shot?"

"I will if I need to, but right now I'm keeping a close watch. Dave's already had her room searched thoroughly. It's clean. He's also Sue's new best friend. I've ordered him to work by her side and not to let her out of his sight." Frank seemed to regain some of his composure, but he looked as agitated as I felt. Would I ever get to see Gloria's spirit? I couldn't stop thinking about the possibility that the entire operation could fall apart at any moment.

"Let's wrap up on the reconnaissance footage." I said.

Once we completed the strategy modifications for Friday's attack, Frank and Clyde accompanied me to the gym where the Fraternity/Cyd Group assault teams were waiting.

"We've concluded our review of the reconnaissance footage and have the intel to adjust your assault team strategies. Frank will hand each of you photo slides and a list of modifications. Clyde will fill you in on what's changed and then you're going to train as if your life depends on it, because tomorrow it does!" I motioned to Clyde and listened as he addressed the group.

"The only thing ya can't be sure of is the security people outside the residence. It could be regular security staff, hit-men, or even agents from the Mexican Cartel."

Today's training would have to do. The Cyd Group was still under my control, to them I was the Red Barron, someone to fear, whatever I asked of them would be carried out without question. The Fraternity members still posed a challenge with their constant barrage of questions, fears, and complaints, but they were now, in all fairness, much more receptive to their missions. As for my own mind, it was cluttered with questions I could not answer. Was I saving Fraternity members or sending them to their deaths? And what about Sue? Whose side was she really on?

I went back to the Bar Room, which was being converted into a command center. It consisted primarily of a long table, three cloned phones set in front of the three chairs Frank, Dave and I would occupy during the attacks. They also brought in one additional chair and cloned phone for emergencies, in case any of the other three mobile phones failed. On the table there was a sheet of paper listing the twenty-four target cities and residences, along with their time zones. I looked over at Frank, who looked worse than the day he showed up at my lake house. This mission was taking its toll on him, on all of us.

"We're as ready as we will be, Frank."

"Let's get some rest Bob. We need to be at our best tomorrow."

I thought about Sue waiting for me. I thought about Gloria. I even thought about Pleasant. This wasn't part of our deal. Everything was supposed to go smoothly, so why was everything so close to falling apart?

When I reached the door to my room I didn't want to go inside. I lingered outside my door, but I knew there was no choice but to fulfill my duty. The Fraternity was counting on me, and even if I often thought it impossible, I was counting on seeing Gloria's spirit when this was all over.

I turned the doorknob, opened the door, and entered my room. Inside were Sue and Dave, Dave having followed my instructions to the letter: *Never let Sue out of your sight.*

"Bob, darling. There you are. Dave has been such a dear, he's seen to my protection all day, everywhere, even escorting me to your room and waiting with me until you arrived. I know this was on your orders, but isn't it possible it's more protection than I need?"

"When it comes to protecting our people, there are no unnecessary precautions, Sue."

"That makes you the most wonderful boss in the world!" she said and beamed at me. Her comment drew a cough from Dave, followed by a slight shake of his head to indicate he had detected nothing suspicious in Sue's behavior.

"I'll take it from here, Dave," I said calmly.

"Thank you for seeing to Sue's safety. I'll see you in the morning at the Command Center." Dave nodded to me, then to Sue, before leaving us alone.

Easing herself onto the edge of my bed, Sue gave me one of her seductive smiles.

"This is our moment, darling, you didn't forget, did you?" she said in a breathy, seductive tone. Her eyes were filled with yearning and anticipation.

"No," I said.

"Good. Come join me." Sue had already removed her light camel jacket and was unbuttoning her blouse when she noticed I was still standing, watching her.

"Why are you not taking off your clothes?"

"I'm sort of shy about it." I said. Sue laughed.

"Oh, hogwash, darling. No stalling on your promise, get undressed."

I slowly and with fumbling effort undressed. I lay the

Sig Sauer pistol I always carried with me on the nightstand. Once stripped down to my Jockey shorts Sue lay on the bed and greeted me with her nakedness.

"You like?" She said in a playful tone as she stretched out her arms and posed for me. I didn't answer. I couldn't answer, and I couldn't take my eyes off of her incomparable figure. Sue's skin was rich and delicate, smooth and firm, dazzling and erotic, without blemish, a perfection impossible to ignore. I lost myself in the slim column of her throat, the swell of her breasts, her enticing naval, the curve of her sensuous waist flowing so easily into the shadow of the pubic curls and finally, her tight hips, thighs, and shapely legs. Sue was a raw, exhilarating, unstoppable force of sexuality. She moved over to where I stood and reached up to pull me down onto the bed. It took all the mental strength I had to pull away from her spell.

"No! I can't do it! I can't make love to you, Sue!"

"Are you too tired? Is that it?" Her expression, a mix of surprise and confusion.

"No." I said.

"Is it because you think we don't deserve this indulgence when everyone else is so uptight about tomorrow?"

"I'm not that noble," I said as I looked into her eyes.

"Well, I'm not what I always appear to be."

An icy coldness spread throughout my body. To me her words were that certainty I was looking for.

Without hesitation, I picked up the pistol and placed the end of its silencer against Sue's forehead.

"You would kill me?" she asked, but there was no hint of worry in her voice. I expected her to beg for mercy or for forgiveness? Her indifference was troubling.

"Yes," I said. A sadness came to Sue's eyes.

"I forgive you. You're doing what you think you should do, but you have a good heart. They ask too much of you." she whispered. I released the safety and placed my finger gently on the trigger.

"Goodbye, my love," she whispered and closed her eyes. I couldn't squeeze the trigger. I needed more than a conclusion of certainty. I needed absolute certainty. I put the safety back on and jerked the pistol away from her forehead. Then I gazed steadily into those tender eyes.

"Are you a spy?" For a moment our eyes locked, then she lowered her head and stared aimlessly at her hands and a tangle of hair fell over her eyes before she looked up at me to respond to my question.

"That's not for me to say."

"Damn it! Why can't you say?" Sue wouldn't answer.

"You're sticking with me until I'm certain you are not a spy. And to make certain you don't have any plans on leaving here tonight, you're sleeping in my bed. Good night Sue." Sue gazed up at me, never looking more beautiful, as her eyes, filled with love, tenderly searched into mine.

"Before I fall asleep, can you hug me and kiss me goodnight?" Taking Sue's pistol and tucking it away, now thinking only of the Sue who had easily enraptured me with her beauty, grace and kindness, I pulled her close to me in an embrace before lightly kissing her lips.

"Good night, my enchanting creature. I've granted your request."

"Thank you, my love," Sue whispered without opening her eyes. I regretfully pulled away from the warmth of her body and her full and moist lips and tucked her into my bed. I laid back on the lounge chair in the corner where I decided I would sleep for the night.

Four hours later, I had showered, shaved, dressed and was back at my work desk studying flight manifests and visualizing the Fraternity/Cyd Group assault teams from strongest to weakest.

Sue woke shortly thereafter and under my close watch she dressed and prepared our morning coffee as usual. The silence between us was palpable, and neither of us appeared to be in a pleasant mood.

"You will stick with me all day, got it?! And with your comforting voice, I can use you on the phones. I'll explain to you what to do on our way to the living room." Sue nodded.

"We have to go." I said.

We headed straight to the living room where the air groups and assault teams were waiting. Eastern Time Zone flights would be the first to depart.

I looked out over the solemn and anxious faces. It was time to rally the troops.

"The day is finally here. You've trained hard and you know what to do. Trust your training, trust your instincts and your partners. And get your asses back here alive and fast." I raised my right fist and shook it vigorously in the air.

"Are you ready?!"

"Yes!" The assault teams yelled back in unison.

"Then go kill those damn bastards!" With more rallying cries the assault teams and air groups shuffled out of the villa and into waiting vehicles acquired to escort them to and from the airstrip.

I looked out a living room window and gazed up at the purple morning sky. The Fraternity members were as ready as they would ever be, but I couldn't help wondering if I was ready? If we failed, was I ready to face the consequences? An involuntary cold shudder made its way up my spine. Then I looked over at Sue, and the chill I felt turned to ice.

CHAPTER 19

WHEN SUE AND I WALKED into the command center, Frank and Dave were already at their seats talking amongst themselves. I motioned for Sue to sit in the emergency seat to the far left and took the one next to hers. Dave shifted in his chair before breaking the silence.

"The waiting begins."

"Let's hope waiting is the worst part," Frank said, glancing uneasily at Sue.

I looked at Sue, hoping to notice a sign of deception so I can finally know for certain if she was a spy, but her eyes only held mine for a moment before looking away.

One hour of waiting, reflecting and wondering led into another, during which Frank, Dave and I kept double-checking schedules and sharing our concerns on the Eastern Time Zone missions we were waiting to hear from.

At 9:30 AM, the cloned phones began ringing. Dave was the first to answer. After a few moments, he announced:

"Resident targets in Boston are dead! Mission a success." Dave reached over and crossed Boston off the sheet of listed cities. Frank and I exchanged a look of relief. Sue's expression was unreadable, but her face had a pallor I'd never seen before.

By 9:45 AM, four more calls had come in, one of them answered by Sue. The assault teams for Washington, D.C., Pittsburg, Detroit and Miami reported their missions as a success. The three remaining EST cities, New York, Philadelphia and Atlanta were each scheduled to report in by 9:50 AM but there was no word yet. What the hell's happening in those cities, especially New York? Cheryl and Giacalone are my strongest assault team. Had Sue warned the targeted residents? How?

As I was pondering this, Cheryl and Giacalone were just stepping out of their mission vehicle. Their air group guard was late because of a blown tire en route to the parking location.

Despite the delay, Cheryl and Giacalone were well on their way to their target location. Following a path along a wrought-iron fence led them to the front of a locked iron gate. On the other side of the gate they could see a flagstone drive, paved through a well-manicured lawn, that led to a large two-story house.

From the reconnaissance footage, Cheryl knew that two Doberman guard dogs roamed the outside grounds, and she came prepared for them. She pulled out a packet of beef flavored dog treats and doused them in Acepromazine, a tranquilizer that would sedate the dogs but not kill them. Dave gave her two doses of the liquid form which would ensure faster absorption into each dog's bloodstream. She slid the treats under the gate while Giacalone waited just a few feet behind her. The plan was to wait until the dogs fell asleep before disengaging the alarm and breaking the lock.

After putting on their masks, Giacalone quietly pushed open the gate. Cheryl quickly scanned the fenced grounds ahead of them. All was quiet.

"Follow me." Cheryl whispered.

"We're late. What if things go sour?" Giacalone whispered, though his brusque voice was still a little loud.

"Then do your best, remember the training." With their Sig Sauer pistols drawn, they passed water fountains and well-manicured gardens as they approached the primary entrance of the property. They inched closer, and Cheryl abruptly changed direction and moved toward the side patio entrance. Giacalone remained several feet behind her, which gave him an unobstructed view of the back and side, but not in time to stop a hulking figure from striking Cheryl's skull with a blunt object.

As Cheryl lay on the ground, her attacker, with a gleaming blade in his right hand, crouched over her and was about to slit her throat when Giacalone fired two shots from his pistol causing the attacker's body to fall sideways and next to Chery's unconscious body.

Giacalone squatted beside Cheryl, his red cheeks puffed out, as he gently shook her on the shoulder.

"Cheryl, ya all right?" he whispered. She didn't respond. He grimaced, and mumbled to himself,

"The Red Baron will have my balls if I let anything happen to ya." He felt a spasm of rage that harm had come to her under his watch.

"Do your best, remember your training." Giacalone repeated those words to himself as he checked her pulse and her breathing and felt relieved, she was still alive.

He thought about the training. The one thing Clyde had hammered on him in the assault simulations was speed. Speed, speed is what you need. Get in and get out as fast as you can.

He knew what Cheryl, what the Red Barron would want was for him to carry on alone. After moving her body to a safer location where he could retrieve her after completing the mission on his own, Giacalone fired a shot just to the side of the patio's doorknob, which shattered the tumbler and bolt locking the door. An accomplished burglar, Giacalone easily made his way through the patio entrance and into the lavishly decorated first floor quarters.

He searched every room on the first floor and found no-one. He then made his way up one side of an exquisite double staircase, with gleaming bannisters.

The top of the staircase led to the bedrooms. He quietly opened the door of the first one he came to and switched on the light. The bedroom was empty, but in the adjoining bedroom he found the Cyprus Group targets, a middle-aged couple arising from bed to get dressed.

Without hesitation, he shot them both through the head. Then having heard Spanish being spoken in one of the other bedrooms off to the other side of the staircase, Giacalone moved toward it, threw open the door, and confronted two startled dark-eyed men in casual clothing. They were dead in seconds.

After searching the remaining rooms and confirming there were no more bodies to claim, Giacalone went back outside to where he'd left Cheryl.

He found her sitting up, exploring her head wound with bloodied fingers. She looked to be in a state of shock and squinting at him as if struggling to see him, she uttered a question.

"You went inside?"

"Yeah, boss. Dose clowns are all whacked. Let's get outta here. Fast! We'll get you patched up later."

Giacalone's hulking figure easily carried Cheryl over his shoulder and quickly got them safely back to the waiting car.

Sue was the one who took the call. After a few moments on the phone, she announced, "That was Giacalone. Mission in New York completed. A success." Then she crossed New York off the list.

Sue still wasn't off the hook, but she wasn't on it either. The uncertainty about her was as perplexing as it was worrisome.

Then I turned my attention back to Frank and Dave, "Has anyone heard from the teams in

Philadelphia and Atlanta?" They both shook their heads.

"Frank, contact the groups sent to those cities and find out what the hell's going on!"

"I tried. I can't contact their air groups, their assault teams or the aircraft. All I get is a buzz of interference on the line."

"Damn!" I looked over at Sue. Every time something went wrong it compelled me to look at her, to look for the slightest sign of deception, but Sue looked back at me in silence, her expression calm and unreadable.

"Almost time for the Central Time Zone air groups and assault teams to take off. They're gathering in the living room." Dave said.

"Hold it!" I said. "Christ, Dave, we don't have enough confirmed returning flights to handle those scheduled for the Central Time Zone."

"Shit! You're right! We'll be one short." We had ten jets available, but we could use only eight of them in the Cyprus Group attacks. We must hold two of the jets in reserve, at all times, for unforeseen catastrophic events. They could be the Fraternity's only means of escape if the Cyprus Group located us and launch an attack of their own. We only had six confirmed aircrafts returning but needed seven for the Central Time Zone operation.

"Dave," I said, with a note of urgency, "we must delay takeoff of one of the Central Time Zone groups until later. Let's make it Corpus Christi. Get over to the CT teams and make sure we put the delay into effect before anyone leaves for the airstrip. Have Clyde and a few of the guards see to it the Cyd Group members returning from their missions are taken to the gym and fed then let them rest. Same for returning Fraternity members. Direct them to their rooms after you've provided whatever special attention they require. And get back here as fast as you can!"

Dave nodded, rose from the table, and left the Bar Room.

For a long while after, Frank, Sue and I sat in the room's silence. No phones rang. Philadelphia and Atlanta still had not called in. Frank smoked and joined me in several cups of coffee. Sue's expression remained benign. Her only activity was drinking the lemonade Bernie brought in for her.

Finally, Frank, unable to remain still any longer, tried once again to reach the Philadelphia and Atlanta groups by phone, but still got no answer.

"They're all dead!" he pronounced fatefully, casting Sue an ill look. Then he looked over at me with a plea of desperation in his eyes.

"You should have shot her! If she's a spy, she's responsible for this!"

"That hasn't been proven," I said, though I secretly harbored the same fear. At that moment, Sue reached over and gently put her hand on mine, then took it away. Was she trying to win me over? Why couldn't she just speak up and put us all out of this misery?

Dave returned to the command center, looking a bit ragged.

"Bob, Cheryl needed medical attention, but the others who have returned seem to be in fairly good shape... a few bruises... but that's all."

"What about the Central Time Zone air groups and assault teams?" I asked.

"They're all in the air... except for the Corpus Christi crew. We should hear from some of them in under an hour. Have you heard from the Philadelphia and Atlanta teams?" he asked, his tone hopeful but laced with worry.

"Not yet. We're still unable to contact them." I said.

"Shit!"

"I don't expect we'll ever hear from them," Frank said, as he once again shot Sue an accusing glance. This time Sue stared back at Frank and again gently placed her hand on mine, just for a moment.

Dave seated himself back in his chair at the Command Center table. At 12:06 PM, as Dave had expected, the phones rang, and reports of successful missions came in. The first of these was Chicago, followed by New Orleans, Houston, then Dallas. A little over an hour later we waited for the St. Louis team to call in, but to no avail. We attempted to make contact but couldn't. The three missions who were MIA — Philadelphia, Atlanta and Saint Louis, had the weakest assault teams, which kept the shadow of doubt on the probability that Sue was a spy.

Dave would soon have the Mountain Time Zone air groups and assault teams in the air. Since this involved only three cities, I had enough jets returning to send the delayed Corpus Christi air group and assault team off with them.

With everyone's nerves already rattled, the waiting began all over again. Sue still seemed perfectly calm and collected. Frank was the most agitated by the wait.

"It may take an hour before we hear from any of them," Frank groaned, his lips pursed, speaking more just to be saying something to cut through the heavy silence. But shortly after, the phones rang. Frank looked puzzled.

"Damn! It's much too early for anyone to be calling in." Dave was the first to pick up. After a few moments of silent listening, he spoke into the mouthpiece, "Jesus...hold on!" Then he gave me a hesitant look, the phone squeezed tightly in his hand. "Bad news on route to Phoenix," he said solemnly, his face suffused with alarm. I shot him a quick grimace.

"Now what?" Holding the phone, Dave eased up out of his chair.

"It's Randy Erickson. His teammate, Joey Nino, just died of a severe stroke. On the plane. Randy has no killer. He refuses to do the killing himself."

"Hand me the phone." I said and spoke into the phone.

"Randy, Bob here. Proceed on to Phoenix. I'll send you a killer pronto who will meet you at the designated landing area. Have the jet you're on fly Nino's body back here, along with the air group member in charge, but keep the air group guard driving the car with you. The guard, you and the killer I'm sending you will fly back on the jet that's leaving now." I paused for a moment. "Got that?"

"Okay. Your new killer is on the way." On disconnecting the conversation, Dave stared at me with a confused expression.

"But, Bob. How can we send him a killer pronto? It will take time dragging one of the returned Cyd Group members out of the gym, and he will be too tired and not know the strategy for Randy's mission."

"But I do," I said.

"You?!" Dave grimaced. "You're Randy's new killer?"

"No. Sue will be his new killer. She's flying with me." If Sue refused to kill the targeted residents on Randy's mission, that would be my proof positive that she was a spy. Sue broke her silence.

"Oh, no! she said.

Dave cringed. "Jesus, Bob. Sue?!"

"That's how it will be," I interrupted, with a tone of finality in my voice.

Frank, with an inkling of what I was up to, smiled with relief, and commented.

"This spy will not be coming back alive." Sue, now out of her chair and on to her feet, spoke again.

"Bob, don't do this." She pleaded. The loveliness of her caressed every bone in my body, but I had to dismiss it.

"You're in no position to refute orders!" I said. Command was a curse. That laid on my mind as I strolled over to a cabinet, studied its contents for a moment, gathered a few items. I handed Sue a pistol.

"It's loaded," I said. Then I handed her a mask and a pair of the gloves. She accepted them with a troubled look but said nothing. Finally, nodding at the clothes, I said, "I think that's your size. You can change on the plane." Then I turned my attention back to Dave.

"Call Scott at the airstrip. I want him to do the flying. Make sure the returned jet he'll be using is refueled and prepared to take us aboard. Have the jet ready to take off by the time we arrive."

Next, I addressed Frank.

"You're in charge of the Command Center until I get back."

Giving me a solemn look, Frank said, "Just get back!"

Dave was on the phone with the airstrip when Sue and I left the Bar Room.

At the airstrip, Sue and I exited the Fraternity limo, which by now I had claimed as my own, then approached a white jet with red trim and climbed onto the lowered steps leading into its cabin. Without a word between us, I helped Sue aboard the aircraft, raised the steps and sealed the door, then escorted her to a soft leather seat in the cabin, dumping the dark leather clothes, masks, and gloves I was carrying, along with some reconnaissance slides, into the seat behind her.

"I'll be back shortly." I said before heading into the cockpit while the engines started revving.

There, facing an elaborate instrument panel with a global position, the jet operating on triple redundancy backups, sat Scott Duhamel, a hardy, well-built man in a blue Fraternity uniform. I knew Scott. He had flown with us for many years. Looking up at me with a familiar smile, he greeted me.

"Bob, it's been a while."

"Been keeping busy, my friend."

"I bet. I hear you're running this place."

"For now."

"That includes me. So, where are we going chief?"

"Phoenix, Arizona." I took out a map and pointing to a marked area on it instructed him on our planned destination.

"You land here, a short distance outside of Phoenix. Our people will wait for us there." Scott studied the map, rubbing his chin.

"Once you land this bird, you will wait for us until we return."

"Roger that, chief."

"How's the weather on the way?" I asked as I handed him the map.

"Clear, once we get over this front."

"We're late, so turn on the burners."

"Roger that!"

"Uh... Scott, do you have a pack of cigarettes?"

"For the lady?"

"No. For me. I know you smoke."

"Yeah, but you don't."

"I'm starting today. Not the best of days." Scott handed me a pack from his shirt pocket.

"Thanks. Let's move!" While the jet was roaring down the runway, I hurried back into the main cabin, to take a seat. When the aircraft was in the air and had leveled off on its destination toward Phoenix, Sue and I, in silence, put on our dark clothes.

I sat on the aisle seat next to her. Her pale face was facing the window. So far, she had not spoken a word to me, and the air in the cabin seemed heavier. We sat there together in silence.

The silence didn't bother me, but to make certain Sue had no misunderstanding about the significance of our journey, I finally said to her:

"You will do all the shooting. If you kill the targeted residents, then I will know you're not a spy. If you refuse to do this, then I will know you are a spy, and I will shoot you." Sue turned to look at me. Her eyes came alive again. The area around the pupils were a sparkling green. She placed her hand gently on my cheek and let the words roll softly from her lips.

"Whatever happens, I love you." She said before taking her hand away from my face and turning her attention back to the window.

I sat back, lit a cigarette and mournfully contemplated whether Sue would have to die today.

CHAPTER 20

THOUGH SUE DIDN'T SPEAK TO ME the remainder of the flight, I continued to explain what we would do once we landed. She kept looking out the window, but I knew she was listening. I kept my tone matter of fact, but it took focus and concentration to keep my emotions in check.

"The target location we're approaching has few obstacles to worry about. With me right behind you, I don't see any reason you can't pull this off," I said.

"Approaching Phoenix," Scott announced over the loudspeaker.

I made my way back into the cockpit and watched as Scott circled a landing area.

"Land this baby, Scott."

"Roger." Cutting the air speed, pulling up the jet's nose in a perfect glide, Scott maneuvered us into a smooth landing. Then the reverse thrust of the engines slowed us down. When we had come to a complete stop, I gave Scott a thumbs up.

"Remember, you wait here until I return." Scott nodded, and I led a silent Sue onto the exit ramp and into a savage heat.

Randy Erickson was in his early 50s. He was lean, near six-foot, and dressed in an impressive tan suit. He watched us deplane, and I could tell from his expression I was the last person he expected to see.

"Bob?! What are you doing here?!"

"Say hello to your new partner." I said and pointed toward Sue.

"Your secretary?!... Your secretary is a killer?! You're shitting me, right?"

"Nope. Rumor has it she's handy with a gun. Plus, she's thrilled about her promotion and always wanted to see Phoenix. Figured let's help her kill two birds with one stone, or one bullet." I said, then let out a chuckle. The situation was preposterous. In some ways, this whole God-damned operation was.

Randy just stood there, staring at me, his expression frozen in disbelief. He brushed his hand through his red hair, as if that would make everything go away.

"We have to get a move on!" I said.

"Okay, yeah, okay." Randy led me and Sue toward the parked blue Mercedes sedan. Frank thought it would blend with the neighborhood's affluence.

Behind the wheel of the Mercedes was the air group's guard, a large-nosed man named Chuck. Randy took the passenger seat, Sue and I sat in the back, holding our masks and gloves in our laps. I watched Chuck's expression through the rearview mirror. My arrival with Sue was raising a lot of questions and none I was in the mood for answering.

"Let's go Chuck, drive!" I didn't have to tell him

again as he stamped down on the accelerator and got us moving.

When we arrived at the designated parking location, Randy, Sue and I exited the vehicle, and as I did with Scott, I reminded Chuck he was to wait for us until we returned. As for Randy, I had to get him up to speed as quickly as possible, seeing as we trained him for a two-person operation not three.

"I'm just tagging along." I said. Randy led the way to within close sight of the target residence. It was a sprawling, one-story mansion with brick patios, solar-green windows and long verandas that stretched along its exterior.

In the back of the property, there were multiple gardens, and a long brick patio overlooking a swimming pool. There were also lounge chairs and tables strategically placed underneath colorful umbrellas that could limit exposure to the scorching Arizona sun.

Turning to Randy, I said, "You wait out here, as a rear guard. Sue and I will handle the inside." Randy shrugged. "Sure." Sue and I slowly approached the front of the property until I signaled for us to stop so I could listen for sounds, but there were none.

"Put on your mask." I whispered, then raised the pistol in my hands and motioned for her to do the same. We made our way up a circular drive with an emerald green lawn toward a large, multi-car garage. Two amber lanterns and an antique, hand-carved Mexican door framed the entrance. We had our backs up against one of the walls of a long veranda.

"We're going in blasting and you're leading the way." I said. "If you don't shoot whoever's inside, then I have no choice but to shoot you."

Sue held my eyes with a look of sorrow. Odd thing was, I got the feeling she was sad for me and not herself.

"Let's go!" I nodded and motioned for her to move ahead.

Holding our pistols in front of us, my finger on the trigger, ready to squeeze, we entered a vestibule, then a much larger room with a pegged oak floor, lavish furnishings of Spanish influence, and a massive mock fireplace. The room was empty.

"Let's find the master bedroom. They're probably holed up in there." I said with a hint of urgency. I wanted to get this over with. See who Sue really was. Once and for all.

I set us off on a brisk pace, passing a long dining room, then a large Mexican tiled kitchen, then an elaborate den. All empty. Finally, we came to a long corridor, leading to other rooms.

"Down here! Quick!" I whispered. The first two rooms were empty. Then we came to what was the master suite and before Sue crossed the room's threshold I said, "Shoot anything that moves!"

Rushing in, ready to fire–at least I was, but we found no one, only a huge-sized bed resting on a floral carpet, the room decorated in blue and white toile, harmonizing with all the other elegant niceties. The suite opened into a glass solarium. It was empty. No one there, or in the sunken bathtub-jacuzzi, or exercise room or the adjoining bath and dressing area with lit floor-to-ceiling mirrors. Where the hell were they?

"Let's search the remaining rooms." I whispered. Again, we found no one. The garage was next; I motioned for Sue to lead the way and unexpectedly found my attention drawn to her well-rounded derriere. What the hell was I thinking?

The garage, like the rest of the residence, was empty. This shouldn't be happening. Something was wrong. Sue, all the while watching me intently, never said a word, not even when I scowled and wondered aloud:

"Where the hell are they hiding?" We'd searched every room. Finally, exasperated, I said to Sue:

"They must be out back!" I opened the glass doors that led to the brick patio trimmed with exotic floral landscaping. The scent was exhilarating. Gloria would have reveled in it.

I scanned everything. The tables, chairs. No sign anyone had been there. What the hell, I mused. I know Cyd's scroll was accurate. I concluded that the targeted residents must still be inside, hiding. Flustered, thrown off balance, unable to think clearly, on impulse I rushed back into the home, and searched every room thoroughly. Still, I found no one.

"These bastards have to be here somewhere." I said. I knit my brows and turned to look at Sue, she wasn't by my side anymore. "Damn, Sue, where the hell are you, Sue?!" I yelled. There was no response.

My breath catching, I hurried out back to the pool area, where I had last seen her. I yelled out her name, but she wasn't there. Then I noticed a folded white paper on top of one of the pool tables. It was a note in Sue's delicate hand.

Not the goodbye you wanted, my darling. I love you.

For a moment, I stood there motionless and numb. Had they set me up? Whether it was from a sudden case of paranoia or my gut telling me I had to get out of there, I don't know. I moved toward the entrance and stepped out, half expecting to dodge a bullet. I got to the circular drive,

Randy was not there, so I walked as fast as I could without attracting unnecessary attention back to the parked Mercedes.

No sign of Randy or Chuck. Were Pleasant and Cyd behind this? Why? Nothing was making sense. We had a deal. If I stay alive, they better damn well keep up their end of the bargain. The keys were still in the ignition, I wearily plunked myself behind the wheel and sped off toward where Scott's jet had landed, praying it was still there.

I got to the jet and felt a surge of relief when I saw Scott waiting. He came out to greet me, sensing something was wrong.

"Where are the others?"

"They didn't make it." I said and hurried onboard the plane. I couldn't explain and I didn't want to.

Once I settled into my seat, I called Dave.

"Dave, it's Bob. Any word on Corpus Christi or the Mountain Time Denver and Tucson teams?"

"Negative. We're still in the dark, Bob! For a minute we thought you were in trouble. Scott said he didn't know where you were. What happened in Phoenix with Sue?"

"Sue's gone, Dave."

"She's dead?!"

"No, gone. As in disappeared, but I don't want to talk about Sue. I need you to send out the Pacific Time zone teams as scheduled. I'm heading back."

"With Sue on the loose, Bob, are you sure?"

"It's an order, Dave, just get it done!"

"Okay. But, Bob, we need six jets but only have four coming back."

"Use the two we've got on reserve. No more questions. Get moving on this!"

"Okay. But Bob, I feel so damn useless and guilty sitting here on my ass while our people are out there suffering and needing my help."

"Damn it, Dave! That's not your mission at the moment."

It was midafternoon by the time I returned to the Command Center, and by then all the Pacific Time Zone teams were in the air. Frank greeted me with a hug and clap on the back. The Arizona heat and all that had transpired in just a few hours left me shell-shocked and I bet I looked it.

"Where's Dave?" I asked. Frank hesitated before answering.

"He's now the assault team Fraternity member heading to San Diego."

"What?! Frank, that's the toughest mission of them all. How did you let this happen?"

"Wendy Warburton got sick shortly before take-off, and Dave took her place. He made the decision without consulting me."

"He knows better than that!" I snapped. "His place is here! In the Command Center! No matter what!" Frank, sighed. "So is yours, Bob. You running off to Phoenix set a terrible example."

"God damn it! I can make that decision. I'm in command!"

"For a while, we thought you were no longer in command, Bob. What happened in Phoenix? What didn't you tell Dave?"

"What happened is nothing happened. There was no one on the property and Sue disappeared. That's all I have to say."

"You think this means the Cyprus Group knows what we're up to?"

"Frank, I don't know. I don't know what to think." I said and watched Frank pace the way he did that fateful day he arrived at my lake house.

"Could Sue be the reason we haven't heard from Denver, Tucson or Corpus Christi? Maybe she somehow got a warning out about the Philadelphia, Atlanta, and St. Louis missions. Maybe the Cyprus

Group intercepted them." Frank stopped pacing for a moment to look at me.

"Bob, do you realize that combined we've lost six missions, and everyone on them is probably dead?" I had no answer.

"Bob, we still have time to recall the Pacific Time Zone teams."

"We're recalling no one! No matter how you look at it, Frank, it is a bloodbath. You told me this was a war. Well, you know what? War is bloody. And after how far we've come, how far you've made me come, I'm not stopping, and neither are you!"

Frank nodded and looking defeated took a seat. Despite what I'd said, I knew there was more urging me to complete the mission than what I'd said. Sue's deception, coupled with the stress of this entire operation, brought my thoughts back to Gloria. She was still the sole motivation for doing any of it. I made a deal, and I was doing everything in my power to deliver so I could see her spirit. Could it be possible that Pleasant was backing out on our deal? Was what happened in Phoenix a really bad sign? Was I meant to fail? Was I some kind of fall guy?

Gods and mortals. Dreams and love. A deadly deceit of life and death. What the hell have I gotten myself into?

CHAPTER 21

CYPRUS GROUP MEMBERS, Rodney and Angela Lovett, had just arrived at their ranch located 30 miles from the outskirts of San Diego when the private line on Rodney's smartphone rang. The call lasted only a few moments and left him visibly shaken.

"Angela, that was Fernando. We're under attack and there isn't much time!"

"What?! Can't we go somewhere? We don't have security. No one will be here until tomorrow. What are we going to do?!"

"Fernando said the cartel has three people that can get here quickly to keep us safe."

"Are they reliable?!" Angela said with a note of panic in her voice. "Who, who are they?"

"I've written their names down. "Salim Abdul Sayyaf, Tawfig al Hazm, and Newaf bin Attosh."

"Arabs? Our lives are in the hands of Arabs?!"

"Fernando says they're tough. The terror of the border. Salim, their leader, is one vicious sonofabitch."

Salim Abdul Sayyaf got behind the wheel of a truck carrying the remains of two Coyote smugglers. He and his accomplices, Tawfig al Hazm and Newaf bin Attosh, had tossed the bodies in the truck's long rear trailer and covered them with a large tarpaulin flap. Salim and his men were in their late twenties, hard faced and battle tested in the Middle East. Individually they were dangerous but working together they were well-coordinated and lethal. They sat side by side in the truck's wide cab as they made their way along a dusty road that cut through the sandy desert landscape. Armed with Mexican semiautomatic military pistols and sheathed knives, their next stop was the Lovett Ranch.

They drove several miles before Salim pulled the truck to a stop on the side of a road. He studied a map for a few moments before turning his attention back to Tawfig and Newaf and switching to Arabic.

"We will arrive in ten minutes," Salim spoke calmly, but those who knew him understood it was the manner with which he delivered warnings.

"There will be no mistakes. You must stick to my plan. We will capture the American assassins, kill them, dump them in the truck, and wipe away any evidence. At the border we find some illegals and dump them in the truck too. When they find the bodies, they will blame the Mexicans. Like I said, stick to my plan. Got it?!" Salim's face was grim. Beneath his glossy black hair, his dark, deep-set eyes were unsettling. Both Tawfig and Newaf were aware of the consequences if they screwed up. Salim had a reputation, and they knew he could live up to it. He switched back to English.

"Do you understand every detail?" Tawfig and Newaf each gave a nod.

"No deviations from my plan," Salim said.

"And speak only English while at the ranch."

Dave's jet was on the final descent to San Diego. He thought about Kym and not letting her know what he was about to do. He didn't want to upset her and there was no way she would have let him come. The Lovett Ranch was by far one of the more difficult targets. The desert eliminated the possibility of using stealth to approach the property. A lot could go wrong, especially since it called for a daring and full-frontal attack.

When the jet landed, while the air group Fraternity member remained inside the aircraft with the pilot, Dave, his Cyd group killer partner, Nino Lasetti, and the air group guard, Smiley, quickly deplaned and hastened toward a parked Pontiac Sedan. The vehicle came fully equipped with bullet-proof windows and tires that could handle a rough drive over the arid landscape. Dave and Nino hopped into the backseat and Smiley drove them toward the ranch.

"Get this mother going at warp speed!" Dave said to Smiley.

Immediately, Smiley had the car racing off on a sandy road. In the backseat, Dave and Nino were busy attaching silencers to their Sig-Sauer pistols.

"We go in guns blasting, no hesitation, then out. And keep a sharp eye for security people." Dave said.

"Yeah," Nino grunted. "I'll blast their asses before they can blink an eye. Can't wait!" It wasn't long before they arrived at a length of fence posts and barbered wire. Smiley brought the car to a stop just where a large blue signed announced: LOVETT RANCH

He crawled the car forward through a gap that led onto a back road. Dust piled up behind them as thermal currents whipped up small stones that began banging on the windshield.

"Can you speed it up?" Dave yelled. "We don't have the time to be going this slow."

"Doin' the best I can, Dave. Dis spot is tough drivin'." They passed some Joshua trees and drove over a rough road covered in thistle, sage and sand before dipping into a small gulch and coming out onto a smoother path. Smiley hit on the accelerator again until a long and low, adobe walled ranch house came into view. The windows and roof of terracotta gleamed in the sunlight. Dave caught sight of a silver GMC Envoy and a large truck with a tarpaulin flap cover on its rear parked in front of the ranch.

"Be prepared for any surprises!" Dave said. "Smiley, if Nino and I aren't out in ten minutes, haul your ass back to the jet."

With their gloves and masks on, pistols drawn, Dave and Nino blasted out of the car and into action. They made it onto the porch where Rodney Lovett opened the door and peeked his head out before ducking back inside. An easy kill, Dave thought.

Dave and Nino pushed their way into the ranch and pursued Rodney into the furnished confines of a sizeable living room, but it was empty. As they looked around trying to decide which direction to go in, a small canister spewing sleeping gas landed in the room and caused them both to collapse.

Salim, Tawfig and Newaf, wearing special gas masks, walked into the room.

"You know what to do," Salim said, his voice muffled through his gas mask. Tawfig and Newaf removed the cannisters, aired out the room, then bound Dave and Nino's hands behind their backs, before removing their guns, and using smelling salts to bring them back to consciousness.

When Dave and Nino came to, they were on the floor, bound back-to-back, and surrounded by Salim, Tawfig and Newaf, who had their guns trained on them. Not good, Dave mused.

"Are you going to shoot us?" Dave asked.

"Now, that would be inhospitable." Salim replied with a sly smirk before his eyes turned cold, hard and menacing.

"But you will, as you Americans like to say, be history soon enough." Nino, inflamed with rage, stared into Salim's eyes.

"Yer the one who will be history when the Red Barron gets a hold of yer ass and skins ya alive!"

"Quiet!" Salim cut him off. "Remain quiet or this will be much more unpleasant."

"Move them outside!" Tawfig and Newaf pulled Dave and Nino to their feet, then, with the muzzle of a gun jabbed into their backs, pushed Dave and Nino forward. Dave's thoughts were racing, nothing went as planned and now he was going to die and Kym was probably never going to forgive him.

Once out on the porch Salim kept his gun on Dave and Nino while Tawfig and Newaf ran to the truck to flip over one end of the flap in the rear trailer. That done they went back to Dave and Nino and once again used the muzzle of their guns to herd them forward. Salim trailed from behind.

As the men approached the truck a black Lexus pulled up and stopped right where Smiley had parked two hours ago. Sherry Whitfield, an attractive, middle-aged blonde, one of the Lovett's friends and neighbor, stopped by for a surprise visit. She knew they were returning today and wouldn't have a cook, so she was bringing her own cook to prepare them a meal. The two women stepped out of the Lexus before they could register what was happening.

"Hey, what's going on here?!" Sherry asked before she noticed the guns and the severity of the situation. She staggered backwards and immediately felt a tremor run through her. Meanwhile, Sherry's cook, a thin, frail woman with gray, blinking eyes, also saw the guns and took a few steps back.

"What, what's happening?" She said with a note of hysteria. Salim speaking in Arabic reminded his men that there are to be no witnesses and that they must take the women too.

Nino taking advantage of the distraction made a break for it and ran, his bound arms making for an awkward getaway. He'd only gotten a few feet before the sharp blade of Salim's knife landed in the back of his neck causing blood to spurt from his body as he collapsed to the ground.

Meanwhile, the cook was frantically and ineffectively trying to create distance between herself and Tawfig who was fast approaching.

"Stay away from me! Stay away from me, please!" She cried out in hysterics, but to no avail, Tawfig dragging her writhing and screaming in the truck's direction. Sherry in shock stood with her back against the black Lexus and seemed unable to move. As Newaf approached her, he let his eyes roam over her body. Under different circumstances, if Salim hadn't been calling the shots, he might just give himself the satisfaction of having her way with her first. Lucky for her there would be no deviation from the plan.

"Don't you dare touch me!" she yelled out. "My husband..."

Newaf clamped his hand hard over her mouth as she continued to let out a muffled scream.

"Put them in the back of the truck," Salim ordered. The women's kicking and screaming did little to stop their captors from manhandling and dragging them to the truck. The cook was the first tossed into the back, quickly followed by Sherry. Neither of the women were aware of the dead bodies lying under the covered portion of the truck's trailer behind them. Tawfig and Newaf then dragged Nino's body before dumping it into the truck.

Salim jabbed his gun into Dave's ribs to steer him forward.

"Your partner is dead. If you resist, the women will be too." Feeling numb and wanting no harm to come to the two women, Dave nodded and allowed Tawfig and Newaf to help him climb into the back of the trailer. Instinctively, they all crouched down low onto the bed of the truck as their captors climbed in after them, pulled down the flap and ushered all of them into immediate darkness. In the absence of light, the first thing to assault their senses was the stench of urine mixed with the smell of human decay. Tawfig clicked on a flashlight and immediately the dead bodies lying in a pool of dried blood came into view. The scene before them induced a mix of shock, horror and terror.

The cook let out one scream after the next while Sherry unable to utter a sound cupped her mouth as she sobbed and hyperventilated all at once. Dave bowed his head, drew in ragged breaths and silently berated himself for his foolishness in thinking he could handle this situation. He was in way over his head. And just when things couldn't seem any worse, the smell of cordite, a smokeless explosive, filled the air. The realization that he was about to die settled in.

Salim, who was sitting quietly until this point, gave a nod of affirmation. Tawfig and Newaf then drew the double-edged Mexican daggers from their sheaths, and in one swift motion, clasped the women's mouths with one hand, and slashed open their throats with the other. Their bodies collapsed like rag dolls. Dave heard the final gurgling signs of life before there was silence and absolute stillness.

Two hours ago, Frank and Bob were in the command center, anxiously waiting for word, when Smiley's call came in.

"Too early to be hearing from any of them," Frank said, almost as if trying to ease his own nerves.

"I know, but mostly I'm concerned about Dave. Of all the targets, San Diego is the most challenging," I said.

"Dave knew that, let's just hope Nino can protect him," Frank said.

"If the Cyprus Group gets wind that we're coming, nothing will save him."

"You should have killed Sue."

I was about to say something when the phone lines started up. I was the first to grab the line. It was Smiley, he was out of breath.

"Boss, I think all hell busted loose! I had a scram outta there and git back to the jet. Dave's orders."

"How long has it been since you left Dave and Nino?"

"Bout ten minutes."

"What's your location, have you returned to the jet?"

"Yeah."

"You stay put. I'm on my way."

I hung up and made another call to the airstrip.

"Scott, I need you to refuel and prepare for take-off, we're going to San Diego."

"Frank, you're in charge until I get back."

"If you get back."

I left the Bar Room and made for the limo that would take me to the airstrip. I was about to climb in when Kym rushed over to me.

"Bob, do you know where Dave is? I can't find him, and I haven't heard from him."

I had no time to explain or be delicate, but she might as well know the truth.

"He's on one of our missions. It was his choice, and I wasn't here to stop him."

"No! Bob, how is that possible? He's not like you! They'll kill him, Bob! Do something!" She shrieked. Her eyes were tearing up and I had no time to console her.

"Kym, I'm on my to help him. That's the best I can do right now." I said, before quickly getting inside the limo.

Once I got on the plane I sat with Scott in the cockpit.

"If you go full blast, how long will it take you to get there?"

"I'd say thirty minutes. What's the hurry?"

"I'm trying not to be late for a party." Scott sighed, "I hope it leaves you in better shape than the last one."

Thirty minutes later, along with the air group's Fraternity member, I sent the jet Dave and Nino had arrived on back to the villa, then Smiley and I scrambled into the Pontiac.

"Smiley, you've already been there, let's haul ass!" I ordered. Smiley pumped his foot down on the acceleration and we were on our way.

"What's the plan, boss?"

"That depends on what's waiting for us. No matter what happens, you do exactly what I tell you, without hesitation." I said while inspecting my Sig Sauer pistol and silencer.

"That mean me killin'?"

"We're not here to sell bibles, Smiley. We need to get Dave and Nino out of there, and if the targets are still alive, it's on us to complete the mission. You have a pistol?"

"Yeah, but I hope you do all the killin'. I hear yer good at that."

"We all have our faults."

When we arrived at the Lovett Ranch, I got out of the car and quickly scanned our surroundings. Then a woman's piercing scream shattered the silence. The sound had come from inside a parked truck parked out front. I motioned to Smiley to lean in close.

"Quick! That truck, throw that tarpaulin back over the trailer as far as you can." I whispered.

As soon as Smiley did what I asked, Newaf who was about to slit Dave's throat looked up with a startled expression. Without hesitation, I fired my pistol. The bullet struck him in his chest, making the knife pop out of his hand as he reeled backwards. In quick succession I fired two more bullets, Salim and Tawfig each getting a bullet to the head.

I handed my gun to Smiley and looked over at Dave, who looked bewildered and exhausted. As soon as Dave realized he was free, he maneuvered his bound body forward over the end of the truck's trailer and attempted to throw himself over the edge. I caught him before he hit the ground.

"Let's get you out of here, Dave."

"Bob... How?" he couldn't finish his sentence. His voice was just above a whisper.

"No need to talk now," I said. "Let's just get you out of here."

"Wait," Dave said, pointing at the trailer. "Nino. His body. It's in there." I grabbed my gun from Smiley, then looked over at the ranch's porch.

"Smiley untie Dave and put Nino's body in the trunk." I turned my attention back to the house. If the Lovetts were still in there, they couldn't have heard the shots fired because of the silencer. Then a movement by the door caught my attention. I saw their heads pop into view for just a second before ducking back inside. I heard Angela Lovett let out a shriek as I ran in after them and fired immediately. They each took a bullet in the back of the head and were dead before their bodies hit the floor.

Not wanting to press my luck, I ran back down the

steps and into the Pontiac. I quickly slid into the back seat next to Dave.

"Get us the hell out of here Smiley!"

"Damn right! Ya don't have to tell me twice."

On the drive back to the jet, Dave was quiet. He still looked disoriented, but finally after a few moments, he mumbled.

"Bob, how? How did you pull this off? Jesus."

"Take it easy, Dave. We can talk later," I said. Then I patted him gently on the knee and let out a sigh of relief. I was so damned grateful he was still alive. Dave looked at me, I'd never seen that hollow look in his eyes before. Whatever happened today got him shook up.

"You saved my ass. You risked your life. They were monsters, Bob!"

"Now don't go making me a hero. I only saved your ass to get Kym off my back." Dave fell silent for a moment.

"I thought I'd never see her again," he said. "Is she okay?"

"She will be." I said.

When we got back on the jet, I called Frank at the command center, but when I punched the numbers all I heard was static on the line.

Then Sue's voice came on the line.

"Commendable heroics, darling! Your five killings today have earned you the honor of being the Cyprus

Group's number one enemy. It would be wise for you to get out of this before you use up your nine lives. Miss you. Love you!" Then static again and the line went dead.

I stood there stunned. What the hell was Sue up to? And why did the sweet rhythmic softness of her voice still stir up something deep within me? Did she mean it when she said she loves me? All these questions, but the biggest of all was how could Sue be at the command center? Was the Cyprus Group at the Villa?

I punched in the numbers for the Command Center again. This time there was no odd static, and no answer. A chill swept over me.

Pressed for help on the phones, Frank had asked Kym to help him in the Command Center. She was there when he received the call from the air group driver on the Los Angeles mission.

"We got in a crazy wreck and totaled our car, sent Brian and Lombardi to the hospital."

"Hell!" Frank gasped.

"Damn lucky I wasn't hurt, snuck away from the police and back to the jet, but it had taken off, and we have no assault team." Frank paused for a moment, desperately trying to collect his thoughts. With Dave and I having set an example for him — as bad as it was, Frank suddenly felt honor bound and compelled to follow it by rising to the occasion. He knew from the air group Fraternity member returning in the jet I had sent back from San Diego that he had an aircraft available he could use.

"Can you get another car?" Frank asked.

"No problem."

"I'm sending you another team. Wait for it at where your jet landed."

"Okay." Placing his mobile on the table, Frank turned to Kym.

"The assault team for LA got into an accident, they're in the hospital. You and I, we have to replace their assault team, Kym." Kym's lovely face morphed into a horrified expression.

"I, I know nothing about shooting a gun, Frank," she objected.

"I'll teach you on the plane. This is an emergency, Kym!" Frank said urgently.

"I will not kill! You can't make me!"

"You will kill," he snapped. That's an order! No Fraternity member is exempt from doing what they must do. I don't like putting you in this position, but I have no choice."

"God forgive me," she whispered. Frank called the airstrip and let them know he was on his way. Then he grabbed two pistols, silencers and whatever they needed for the mission. They left the command center unattended.

CHAPTER 22

THREE MILES OFF THE CALIFORNIA COASTLINE, the sun's rays fading into the dimming glow of dusk, a 45-foot sloop splashed through the water on a northern journey, its bow swiftly cutting through the rise and fall of the waves, the wind gust making for perfect sailing.

Sue was on board that sloop, standing on its deck, the wind dancing with her hair, caressing it into lovely twists. A dignified-looking man, well-dressed in sailing apparel, wearing a captain's hat, was standing on the deck beside her.

"Seattle might be interesting," the man said. Sue nodded, looking out over the sea.

Five kills in one day left me feeling only the scars of war and questioning whether I could ever aspire to feeling a sense of dignity or justice.

When Dave and I entered the Bar Room, we found it empty. The realization that no one had manned the command center filled me with a sense of foreboding. I got Bernie on the phone.

"Where the hell is Frank?! Or anyone else who should be here?"

"Don't ask me, boss. All I know is Frank just scrammed outta here somewhere with Kym." Hearing that, Dave froze. "Kym? Where did they go?"

"I dunno."

"Who did Frank leave answering the phones?"

"I guess nobody."

"Damn!"

"Where would Frank be taking Kym?" Dave asked after hearing my end of the conversation. I threw up my hands. "I wish I knew, Dave."

This entire operation was taking its toll on both of us. Dave still looked unraveled by the day's events. I turned over everything I could find in the Command Center, hoping Frank left me a note. There wasn't one.

I sighed uneasily. Then I tried phoning Frank on his cell. No answer. Just then, Bernie came in to check on us.

"Everything okay? Boss?"

"Aside from Frank taking off with Kym, have you noticed anything strange happening around here?"

"Strange? Like what?"

"Like Sue being here or strangers trying to bust in."

"Sue?" he said, slowly shaking his head.

"Nope. Not seen her. No strangers either. If any tried bustin' in, dey would have been shot. We ain't shoot nobody.

"You okay, boss?"

"Dave and I are tired and hungry. Can you get us some coffee and something to eat from the kitchen?"

"Sure thing, Boss!" When Bernie left, I looked over at Dave again. He was sitting with his head in his hands and looked as helpless as I felt at the moment. We were playing the waiting game once again.

"You up for working the phones?" I asked. He looked at me without saying a word. I could see the agony in his eyes. Kym being out there facing the same danger he almost succumbed to was probably too much for him.

I sighed. "Look, right now the phones are not ringing. We could use this time to search for Frank. If we find Frank, we find Kym."

"Yeah, okay, Bob. Let's work the phones." We tried countless times to reach Frank but made no contact. When a call finally came in, it was from Stuart Lee, the Seattle assault team Fraternity member.

"Bob, damn, we just crashed! Engine malfunction, probably too much workload for this old jet."

"Oh, hell Stu! Are you? Is everyone okay?"

"The air group member, guard and pilot escaped with minor injuries. I'm a little more banged up, and my teammate Gallo, he didn't make it. He's dead. What do you want us to do?"

"I will text you a number. Call it! Give whoever answers my name and Frank's name. They will help in dealing with the crashed jet, authorities and every-one else involved. They'll get you back here and deal with Gallo's body. Bring Gallo's pistol back with you."

"Thanks, Bob," Stuart sighed in relief. "I'm sorry the Seattle mission failed." I paused. One thing requiring no thought was my powerful feeling that no matter what, I would keep my end of the deal with Pleasant.

"Stu, I'll take care of Seattle." When I hung up, Dave stood up, in an obvious state of alarm.

"You are not going to Seattle, Bob!"

"I'm going to Seattle, Dave," I said calmly. "You're in charge while I'm gone, and I want your ass to stay put! No more foolish heroics. I need you here, in the Command Center, handling the phones in whatever way you are able. And that's an order!

"Damn, you're not up to it, Bob. You're pushing your luck. They will kill you!"

Before takeoff, to calm some of my anxiety, I went into the cockpit to talk with Scott. Stuart's engine malfunction was bothering me. In preparing for today, we had considered what could go wrong with the enemy. Not for a moment did I expect one of our jets would experience engine failure.

"Scott, tell me about this jet? You think we have anything to worry about? Stuart's plane just crashed from engine malfunction."

"This baby has two new engines. No worries there. Look, no way to account for everything, but we've got a good bird Bob." Scott reassured me.

"Stuart was on one of our older models. The engines likely gave way to overuse, but we won't know for sure until they're done investigating the crash. The pilot, Ben, is a close friend of mine, he's an expert pilot."

"Probably why he survived, and I'm glad he did. We're doing what we can to get him back here."

On route to Seattle, I settled into a window seat and looked out at the stars. The view of the night sky gave me the sense of calm I desperately needed.

There had still been no word from Denver, Las Vegas, San Francisco, Portland, St. Louis, Corpus Christi, Philadelphia, and Atlanta. A hell of a lot of missions, and a lot of people who counted on me and the mission to keep them alive. When I tallied up the Cyprus Group confirmed body count, was it enough for Pleasant to keep his end of the deal? Would I finally get to talk to Gloria's spirit?

"Seattle coming into view," Scott announced over the intercom. From the coordinates I had given him, Scott set the jet down smoothly on a small strip on the outskirts of Seattle. It was 12:46 PT; we were three hours late in arriving, but thankfully, a black Buick Sedan, the mission car was still there.

"Be ready for a quick departure when I return," I said before getting on the exit ramp.

"Roger that. You sure you're okay, Bob?" I didn't respond. The only thing I was sure about was the mission. I had to complete it at all costs.

The doors to the Buick were unlocked, and the key to the ignition was in the glove box. I drove carefully to avoid arousing suspicion with too much speed. The target residence was on top of a hill, perched like a miniature castle. The lights were on inside. My gloves helping me clutch at the steep incline as I climbed up the hill. When I reached the top, I stopped to catch my breath. I checked my weapon and approached slowly. Then, standing outside a window, I noticed something unexpected. There were voices and music playing. A party or celebration of some sort. How could this be? I stood motionless and listened. There was a clinking of wine glasses, a man and woman in conversation. They knew about the Seattle flight crash. Then another man's voice came into the room.

"Fools!" he scolded. "Not the time to ease up on your guard. They always send a backup. They wiped out our people in San Diego. You should not have dismissed your regular security details. I need to get you out of here now!" I made my way over to the garage. A car engine was revving and then I saw a red Maserati Quattroporte back out and idle in the driveway as the Cyprus Group targets, a man and a woman, got into the car's back seat.

By the garage light's illumination I could see a Mexican man was behind the wheel. I moved away from the glare of headlights and felt a cramp in my left leg. I was running out of time, so I raised my pistol and fired several shots at the car's windshield. The driver's body jerked backwards from the force of the bullet. The car lurched forward and crashed into a tree, the engine still grinding.

My leg cramp forced me to hobble over to the car. I opened the passenger door and without hesitation shot the couple buckled into the backseats. I should have stopped after two bullets, but clear thinking evaded me. I kept firing until my pistol's magazine was empty. I had no more cartridges.

I slammed the car door shut and took a moment to lean up against it. I was so God damned tired; I had to move, but I needed a moment. Then I heard a noise coming from the garage and turned to look. Immediately, the fatal flaw in what I had just done entered my consciousness. A tall, dark-skinned Mexican, his eyes glowering at me, stood with his pistol ready to fire. With no bullets left, I knew my luck had run out. So be it.

Then, before I could blink, he was on the ground. Someone had shot him in the head.

"What the...?" From the shadows a figure in dark clothing, with a pistol in hand, emerged.

"Sue?!" Sue strolled over to me, moving with her usual willowy grace, her beautifully symmetrical face filled with radiance.

"I could not watch you die." She said, her voice soft.

"What will happen to you when they find out what you've done?"

"Let me deal with that," she smiled. "You're down to your ninth life, darling. Savor it." Maybe it was the close brush with death that made me think of it, but I couldn't resist.

"How about a kiss then? To begin the savoring."

"I'd like that," she said as she tilted her head up in

expectation. We began with a tender kiss, but quickly it escalated into a fiery, passionate exchange between us. Her delicate fingers rubbed through my hair as I slid a hand down the supple lines of her body.

None of it made sense, but there we were. Amidst the chaos of all that was happening, this one merciful exchange offered the splendor of the heavens and all I could do was surrender. We both did. Then, regretfully, Sue ended the kiss and broke the spell.

"I must go now, darling. Remember, I love you." Then she was off. I stood there watching her disappear back into the shadows. I looked at the carnage around me and felt the sudden urge to get out of there as quickly as possible. I began the arduous descent down the hill, grateful the cramp in my leg had eased up. Disturbing thoughts and questions circled my mind. None of what I could think of made sense. Sue being here, the connection to the Cyprus Group, the repercussions of what happened tonight? The hell with it. There was no thinking through any of this.

When I drove up to the jet and wearily stepped out of the car, Scott who had deplaned rushed up to me.

"Bob, what took you so long? Dave's been calling, nonstop. I didn't know what to tell him."

"I had a close call, but the targets are dead. Let it go at that."

"All right, glad you made it back."

Once back on the plane, sitting in my cabin seat I called Dave while Scott was busy with his pre-flight check. Dave answered on the first ring.

"Dave."

"Bob! Thank God, you're alive!" Dave said.

"Sorry Dave, I couldn't get back to you. Have you heard from anyone?"

"Not yet. I tried to make contact, but they answered none of my calls."

"What about Frank?"

"No."

"Damn!" Why didn't anyone reach the command center? What was stopping them from making contact? Pleasant and Cyd had made it seem like things would go much more smoothly than this.

"You still there?" Dave asked nervously.

"Yeah, I'm here, just thinking."

"Well, I wish you would think your ass back here while you still have one."

"Not yet Dave, I want to drop in on Portland while I'm in the neighborhood."

"Bob! No, are you out of your mind?"

"I just want to have a look, not engage, okay?" I heard Dave let out an exasperated sigh. "I'll call you later."

"Scott, Who's the pilot on the Portland mission?"

"I believe that's Damian McGee. Yeah, him, I'm sure."

"Contact him." Scott tried to radio in Damian's aircraft but after several tries, he gave up.

"Hell, Bob, can't reach him. That's kind of strange."
"Let's get in the air and go look at his landing site."
"What's up?"
"Hopefully nothing."

When we reached the Portland jet's landing location, we found only a car parked nearby.

"Set her down, Scott. I want a closer look on the ground."

"You sure it's safe to land here?"

"Yes. Anything bad should have happened already."

"I hope the hell you know what you're doing!"

"So do I," I mused, hoping I could muster up enough energy for what I have in mind. I had plenty of ammunition onboard the jet, so I reloaded my Sig Sauer magazine and stowed some extra cartridges in my pocket. I had no intention of using the pistol; I was thinking reconnaissance. But I was a quick study and don't intend on getting caught without ammunition twice in one day.

"Wait for me here." I said.

"Okay, chief. But whatever you must do, can you do it quickly? Got a bad feeling about this place." I deplaned and walked over to the parked Ford sedan. It didn't look like anyone had been in the car. I recalled Misha Knight was the assigned Fraternity assault team member for this mission. Where the hell was she?

When I arrived at the target destination, I parked

close enough to set off at a leisurely stroll. There appeared to be no security on the property's perimeter and the home itself was a beautiful, two story structure. As I got closer, I noticed the lights were on inside. I heard loud music and the sound of people gathered for a party. Outside there was a veranda, and a few people were milling about, drinks in hand. For some instinctual reason I felt I could get away with it, so putting on my most charming smile, I boldly walked up the steps onto the veranda and stopped at the edge of the party.

A stout, older gentleman with graying hair, carrying a tray of drinks, greeted me the moment I entered.

"Welcome to our festivities. Would it please you to have a martini?"

"Why thank you." I realized my wardrobe wasn't exactly fitting for the occasion, but perhaps I could blend in as one of those eccentric millionaires who took great liberty in their manner of dress. When a second server with a tray of hors d'oeuvres approached, I relaxed. If they were unperturbed by my appearance, I figured there was nothing to worry about.

Standing outside, sipping on a martini, I quietly looked at the others. These people were in a joyful mood. Behind me I heard bottles of champagne popping, laughter and happy voices. They were celebrating. How can this be?

Then I saw her, a face I recognized. A blonde woman with flashing blue eyes curled under the arm of a tall, gray-eyed man with a robust build. They were the Cyprus Group targets. How could Pleasant and Cyd let them off the hook? What the hell was going on? I was missing something. The pieces just didn't fit.

Then I noticed another couple. The man, swirling French brandy in a sniffer, then taking a sipping swig, flashed a wide crooked grin as he raised his drink in a celebrative gesture.

"Here's to having them by the balls. We will crush them!"

"That will be a glorious day!" the woman smiled. Then after a pause, she said, "Let's dance."

"Lead on, my sweet." The man said as he wrapped his arms over the woman's waist and pulled her close.

A Cyprus Group celebration. Had I been double-crossed? Was I played for a fool thinking the Cyprus Group the intended targets when all along it was me and the Fraternity? I collected myself and nonchalantly strolled out of the party.

As I drove back to the jet, I had the worst premonition. The Cyprus Group would win this war.

Scott was once again waiting just outside the jet.

"You don't look so good, Bob."

"Take me back, Scott. I need to go back." I muttered.

CHAPTER 23

I WAS BACK IN MY SEAT by the window when Scott came out of the cockpit.

"There's a refueling stop about fifty miles from here. I've radioed them to let them know we'll be there shortly." He paused for a moment. "Frank did a stellar job organizing our fuel stops."

I managed a nod. And at the mention of Frank's name, I felt the sudden jab of reality. We were at war and we were losing. And I still didn't know where the missing Fraternity members were.

"Frank." I said his name out loud.

"Get some rest, Bob, you damn well look like you need it." Scott sighed.

"I wouldn't trade for your job if they gave me a million dollars!"

"You're a smart man, Scott."

We were in the air for only a short while, but long enough to continue reflecting on all the loose ends. And for the first time since taking on the mission, I considered the possibility that I could very well die at the hands of the enemy. I thought about Pleasant. The deal we made, the conversation we had, and how I felt a sense of invincibility. I expected things to go wrong; but I didn't expect to fail.

Scott descended onto the landing strip and close to the refueling pumps was a small one-story wooden structure with a sign above it, WELCOME REST STOP!

Maybe I was imagining it, but the place had a peaceful allure to it, so I wandered inside. The interior was shabby, quiet and empty. I picked a corner stool and sat down. I closed my eyes for a moment and just listened to the stillness of the place.

"What will you have, honey?" a woman's voice startled me. When I opened my eyes, I saw her. She had a lovely golden complexion set against blonde hair, an oval face, a disarming smile, and beautiful blue eyes that seemed to sparkle. I couldn't help wondering how such a beautiful creature could waste any of her time in a place like this.

Then I noticed she was holding her right arm down to her side, as if holding a gun.

My mind raced and calculated all the possibilities. Sue knew all the refueling locations, she'd typed them up for the air groups. If the Cyprus Group gained access to that information, then none of the refueling stops were safe. They could make us easy targets. All these thoughts circled my mind as I raised my pistol and shot the woman between the eyes. She fell back and the pistol she was holding dropped from her hand. I ran out.

Outside, I didn't see Scott. I saw two men pushing our jet. I shot them both. A third man came running toward me, while he was drawing a gun from his belt, I shot him too. Then a fourth man upon seeing his friends lying on the ground retreated and scrambled out of sight.

When I found Scott, he was lying on the ground, gagged and squirming, with his hands tied behind his back. He was attempting to speak, his eyes bulging from the effort it took.

I cleared his mouth so he could talk and got to work untying his hands.

"Damn it! Scott will you hold still so I can untie you?"

"Bob what the hell's going on?"

"We caught ourselves in a war zone. You're lucky they didn't kill you!"

"Jesus God Almighty!" Scott shouted. He got up from the ground, clenched and unclenched his fists, trying to get his blood flowing, and darted his eyes frantically about.

"Those guys on the ground, dead?"

"They're not praying," I said, as calmly as I could.

"We're safe for the moment, but we have to get out of here, now!" Scott brought his trembling fingers into my line of sight.

"You see that? I can't fly yet, Bob. I need to calm down."

"The hell with that," I countered. "There's no time. Pull yourself together, refuel the jet, and I'll stand watch. That's an order!"

"You're ordering me to crash?!"

"Scott, if you don't get us the hell out of here, we'll both be dead."

Bruno Ottis — short in stature, thick neck, dark eyes sunk in a stony face, the air group guard whom had phoned Frank about the screwed up LA mission, already shaken by the day's turmoil, found no comfort in watching Frank and Kym exit the jet.

"Frank, I didn't expect to see you."

"We're your assault team. This is Kym, she will replace Lombardi."

Bruno glanced at Kym, then back at Frank as if he was being pranked.

"Wait a minute, she's just a kid, she don't look like she can kill a fly."

"Kym was the only one available, and this is an emergency." Frank said.

"Did the boss man go along with this?"

"Bob's off on a mission. In his absence I am the boss, and I am here to see that this mission is damn well completed."

"But..."

"Enough Bruno! Shut up and let us get on with it, or I'll kick your ass from here to Sunday!"

"If that's yer order, but I'd save kickin' ass for the targets." Bruno led Frank and Kym to a year-old beige Lincoln, then got in behind the wheel. Frank and Kym climbed into the back seat. During the drive, Kym was silent. She kept her gaze out the rear window and focused on the bustle of traffic, and the crescendo of sirens in the distance. She was pale, withdrawn, and visibly agitated but wouldn't utter a single word.

When they reached their destination and got out of the car, Frank pulled her aside. They stood in an affluent neighborhood surrounded by beautiful homes. On an ordinary day, they could be two people out for a walk. But this was no ordinary day. Frank looked into Kym's eyes, with an almost fatherly concern.

"If you have anything you want to ask before we go in there, now's the time," he said.

Kym shook her head. She couldn't seem to look into Frank's eyes. Instead, she nervously scanned their surroundings.

"Then you're ready?" Kym didn't answer.

"Do as I do, Kym. Stay close and we'll do this together." They walked one full block before realizing they were being followed. Frank grabbed hold of Kym's left arm and maneuvered her to turn around with him. They met with the face of two menacing men.

"Kym, shoot now!" Frank ordered.

Just as Scott roared the jet down the fuel stop's runway into a hard wind, Cyprus Group reinforcements arrived and began firing heavy ammunition at the aircraft. Bullets ricocheted or pierced through the jet's exterior. But somehow Scott, with frayed nerves and all, maneuvered the jet into an awkward climb.

"Goddamned slimy bastards!" Scott cursed. Meanwhile buckled into my cabin seat closest to the cockpit, I figured it was a toss-up whether we would make it out of this alive.

"I just hope they don't have heat-seeking missiles." I said.

"Whoa, did you just say missiles are on the way?! Damn it Bob, are you telling me we will get blown to pieces?"

"Calm down, Scott. If they had missiles, they would have used them by now."

"But what if you're wrong?!" Scott shouted. "My God, Oh my God!"

The jet's nose plunged into a nosedive. Scott was losing it, I had to talk fast.

"Scott! You can do this! Get a grip and get us the hell back to the villa, I'm counting on you." Scott fought at the controls and pulled the jet out of the dive, but his flying was erratic. The aircraft jerked unevenly through the night sky. I unbuckled my seatbelt and held onto whatever I could as I made my way into the cockpit.

"Okay, Scott. You're a damned good pilot, and I know you will get us back safely. You can do this!" I took one glance at Scott and could tell my words weren't registering. I buckled up, and one terrible thought entered my mind. We're not going to make it!

Dave was alone in the command center and becoming increasingly agitated. He had to find Frank, but how? The only explanation for Frank and Kym making such a hasty departure was a mission gone wrong. But which one?

He scanned over the Pacific Time Zone missions listed on the sheet. They had crossed San Diego and Seattle off as a success, and Dave knew I was attending to Portland. That left San Francisco, Las Vegas, and Los Angeles. Someone from one of these cities must have called in. And if they did, then Kym was as good as dead. That final thought was too much for him. Dave doubled over and vomited all over the floor before stumbling into the Bar Room toilet to regain his composure.

I considered it a miracle of sorts. It seemed to take an interminable amount of time, but Scott eventually got his mind into a zone and once again had full steady control of the jet.

"Bob, bring me some hot coffee, and keep it coming!" That was the first coherent statement Scott had made since takeoff. If the man wanted hot coffee to keep this bird in the sky, I was all for it. I dutifully dashed back and forth even as I struggled to keep my balance between the cockpit and the galley. After taking an aspirin and a few cups of coffee, Scott needed to use the restroom. He put the plane on auto pilot, and I sat in the cockpit watching the instrument panel for any critical changes. From where I sat, I could hear Scott vomiting, but when he returned to the cockpit, he looked more like his old self.

"Chief, I'm embarrassed. I'm sorry for how I reacted and what I put you through."

"No need to apologize, Scott. This entire operation is more than any of us bargained for." Scott's eyes brightened, and he managed a smile.

Once Scott was in full control of the plane and his emotions, I went back to my window seat. Again, I looked out at the stars and allowed myself to contemplate the predicament I was in. The predicament we were all in.

How much time did we have before the Cyprus Group struck again? Hours, days? They backed us into a corner. What could I do to prevent any further loss of life? Cyd made it perfectly clear I would have no more dreams until this was over. His words circled in my mind, "You are on your own until all the Cyprus Group targets are dead." I had to warn Dave.

They could attack the villa at any moment.

I turned on my mobile and punched the number to the command center. Dave answered right away.

"Dave, it's Bob. Listen, I need you to prepare…"

"Bob!" Dave interrupted. "I know where Kym and Frank are."

"What?!" I said as I instinctively sat up straighter.

"The original jet for the LA mission just returned. The pilot said Frank and Kym flew there on another jet to complete a bungled mission. I'm taking the returned jet to LA to save Kym. She doesn't stand a chance."

"Dave, No! You are not to go! We have vital problems, and, I need you at the Command Center until…"

"Jesus, Bob!" Dave cut me off mid-sentence. "Don't you get it! Kym needs me!" Dave disconnected the line. When he did, I could feel the adrenalin shoot through me. I waited a moment before phoning the command center again. This time Bernie answered.

"Yeah?"

"Where's Dave?"

"He took off, boss. Told me to answer the phone."

"Look, Bernie, I want you to find a Fraternity member and have them answer the phones. You got that?"

"Uh… yeah, boss."

"Then get your ass moving!"

"Scott, you know the name of the pilot originally scheduled for the LA mission?"

"Yeah, it's Doyle McKever. What's up?"

"I need to speak with him. Get Doyle on the radio."

Once Doyle was on the radio, Scott said to him. "The chief, Bob Daniels, wants to chat with you."

"Doyle, Bob here, is Dave Rammairone aboard your craft?"

"He's holding a gun to the back of my head," Doyle answered, his voice controlled but agitated.

"Shit!" Scott shrieked. I held up my hand for Scott to remain quiet.

"Dave has been expecting your call," Doyle continued. "He will allow you this one contact, no more. He won't let me return to base or alter my course and says for you not to try and stop him." What love causes a man to do, I mused. But Dave was right about one thing: Kym doesn't stand a chance. Does Dave? Then I heard Dave's voice over the radio speaker.

"Goodbye, Bob." Then all we heard was silence.

"Bob, everything and everyone is out of control! What do we do now?"

"All you have to do right now Scott is get us back to the villa."

CHAPTER 24

I SAT IN THE CABIN, fighting to keep my mind from becoming unhinged. The weight of pending doom had entered my mind, and I couldn't shake it. I wanted to finish the mission even though I was becoming convinced we were losing or perhaps we had lost, and all my efforts were now futile. An overwhelming sense of guilt took over, and I felt responsible for all the lives potentially lost.

Even though the Fraternity members, and Vocarro's men as well, were Pleasant's pawns, as I was, I could see no other course but to continue forward. The Fraternity members still stood for something, whether it be nobility, honor or justice, or all three. Until my last breath, I will remain devoted to these aspirations. The next step was to contact the command center. My mind made up I dialed the number.

Jon Pascal, an assault member from one of the earlier successful missions to Miami, answered.

"Jon, it's Bob."

"Bob, what's going on? Bernie insisted I answer the phones. Said it was on your orders. But all hell is breaking loose."

"Have you heard from Dave or Frank?"

"No calls. And I don't expect any."

"Why do you say that Jon?"

"Because they're all probably dead, Bob! Gary, Vic, Anna, they haven't returned."

"The other members are afraid. They think the missing are dead too. What are you doing to find them, Bob?" I didn't know what to say, and it was becoming difficult to fight off the feeling of dread and the weight of all the lives held in the balance.

"Jon, let me get back to you."

"No, Bob! You can't leave us hanging! The members want answers, they deserve answers."

"Goodbye for now, Jon."

I immediately cut off our conversation and turned off my phone. Then the dam of emotions broke loose inside me. I'd held it together so long and now I just couldn't see my way out of this situation. The world is fucked and there is nothing I can do about it. I sat in my misery.

"Holy shit!" Scott yelled from the cockpit.

"What's happening?" I unbuckled my seatbelt and hurried into the cockpit. I followed Scott's line of sight and then I saw it. A jet, one of ours, was flying almost parallel to us.

"You think it will shoot us down, Bob?!" Staring at the jet with incredulous disbelief, I couldn't summon a response. A series of intermittent lights began flashing into the night sky.

"That's... that's Morse Code," Scott said.

"Can you read it?" I asked.

"Yeah, hang on. It says to turn on our radio to the Fraternity frequency."

"Then do it!" When Scott tuned on the Fraternity frequency, a clear, firm, feminine voice came over the radio speaker.

"Follow this aircraft, then land behind it. Only Bob is to deplane. Acknowledge." I recognized the voice immediately. It was Sue. My mind sifted through all the recent exchanges we'd had. Our kiss, her words, the way she saved my life.

"Scott, acknowledge the request."

"With all due respect Bob, like hell I will! I'm not falling for that trick. This time, they'll kill us for sure!" Sue's voice radioed in again.

"No harm will come to either of you, Scott. After I speak with Bob, you will be free to depart without further hinderance. Please acknowledge."

"Who's flying your aircraft?"

"That's not important," Sue responded.

"Sue will keep her word. Acknowledge! That's an order!" Roger gave me a dogged look before begrudgingly responding.

"Roger your request. Will follow." Sue's jet flew just ahead of us, heading north along the California coastline. Ten minutes into our pursuit, we heard Sue's voice again.

"We're landing just ahead. Follow us down." Sue's jet descended onto an abandoned airfield. Scott scanned the horizon on the lookout for anything suspicious, but there were no signs of foul play.

After we touched down, I saw Sue's Learjet 45M. It was definitely one of ours. I exited and watched her deplane and approach. The moon and stars were still lighting the sky and for a moment all I could do, all I wanted to do was watch her body move.

With the grace of a dancer, her hair swirling around her lovely face, she walked toward me, and it felt like we were the only two people left. Two people fighting forbidden urges, and it was all that held meaning in this chaotic world. When she was close enough to touch, she flashed me a crushing smile and a look of tenderness as she took my hand and embraced me with all her warmth.

"You do not know what I risk in doing this, darling, with what's in store, but I wanted my farewell to you to be in person."

Then she kissed me with such passion all I could do was surrender to her and to the moment. This was an interlude, a moment of merciful bliss amidst an otherwise chaotic and miserable situation. Slowly, regretfully, we eased out of our embrace.

"Oh, how I love you, my dear man." Sue said in her most tender voice while placing a hand gently on my face. Her lovely antelope eyes searched mine, and the sadness I saw in them was almost too much to bear.

"We will never see one another again, will we," I said.

"This is as it has to be my love. This is our farewell." She kissed me again, this time on the cheek, then whispered in my ear, "Goodbye, my sweet darling. I love you always." Then taking a step back, she added, her tone careful.

"There will be a full-scale attack on the villa at sunrise. I must go, darling." Before she turned away all the sorrow of the world seemed to be in her eyes. I watched her walk away and disappear into the jet. It wasn't until she was once again lifted into the sky that I could register the finality of what happened between us. She'd left and took her love and a part of me with her. The thought of never seeing her again or feeling the way she made me feel amplified the turmoil I was already in.

I had to get back to the Villa. There was no time to dwell on my sadness. I slowly boarded the jet, pulled the steps up, and went back to the cockpit. Scott seemed more at ease and I wanted him to stay that way. I kept Sue's warning to myself.

"Okay, Scott! You know where to go. Let's get there as fast as we can."

As soon as Scott started the engines, I phoned the Command Center.

"Why in hell did you hang up on me?!" Jon yelled into the phone.

"Jon, I need you to listen! You're all in danger. You must evacuate everyone before sunrise."

"Are you crazy, Bob! How am I going to move that many people out of here at once?"

"If you'll just listen to me, I'll tell you how." I said, then gave him a moment to pull himself together.

"Within ten minutes, after I hang up, you will receive a call from one of my associates at Jacob Enterprises. In anticipation of an ambush, I made prior arrangements to facilitate a fast evacuation. All you need to do is assemble everyone, even Vocarro's associates, into the main hall and have them ready to leave. They will fly all of you north into Vancouver. The Cyprus Group won't dare follow you into Canada."

"You got all of that?"

"Yes, yes, I got it!"

"And Jon, let me be clear, if there is any delay it will cost lives."

"And what about you, Bob?"

"Don't worry about me. I can take care of myself. Leave my limousine parked near the airstrip for when I arrive."

"What do you mean for when you arrive? Aren't you flying to Vancouver too?"

"Like I said, I can take care of myself."

"Alone? Against the Cyprus Group, Bob?"

"That's my worry, not yours. Your only concern right now is the lives I'm leaving in your hands. There's not much time left, I need you to move Jon."

"Okay, okay, I got it!" After I disconnected the call, I leaned back in my seat and allowed a feeling of peace to wash over me. This was my last move. My last attempt to save lives.

The only thing left for me to do was to face the inevitable consequences for my unpardonable failure to the Fraternity. Even if some of them lived, I still failed.

By the time we were in descent to the villa's airstrip, we had missed the sunrise, but not by much. I walked into the cockpit wanting a better view of what waited below.

"Bob, something strange going on. I radioed the control tower and got no response. And look, look for yourself, no people, no other aircrafts, where the hell did everybody go?"

"Scott, I need you to listen to me. The Cyprus Group will raid the Villa and I don't want you getting mixed up in all of this. I want you to stop just long enough for me to get off, then get your ass out of here and off to the nearest commercial refueling station. Get enough fuel to reach Vancouver. That's where everyone is."

"Bob, you can't be serious. You want me to leave you here. I can't do that!"

"You can and you will. That's an order!"

"Okay, then."

"That's more like it. And Scott, I will remain ever grateful for your loyalty. I couldn't have done any of this without you."

Scott did as I asked. As soon as I got off the jet, he once again revved up the engines and was back in the air.

I saw no one but found the limousine near the airstrip as I'd asked. Then, as if getting myself worked up for a confrontation, I looked around, mumbling to myself as I strolled toward the car. "Come on. Quit stalling. Come out of hiding and let's get this skirmish over with." But no one made an appearance. They'll get me at the villa, I mused.

Sliding behind the wheel of the limousine, the keys in the ignition, I drove straight for the villa. As I approached the drive, the serene beauty of the place struck me. The sky, streaking with the red and golden hues of morning, was stunning, and served as a fitting backdrop to the mystical magic of this place. I couldn't imagine the end of a war occurring here amidst the chirping of birds and the warm caress of a gentle breeze. They must be inside, I thought. That's where I'll meet my end.

I had every intention to die fighting. I was ready to face whatever awaited me behind those doors. Perhaps the despair of losing Gloria and now Sue had anesthetized me just enough to face whatever lie ahead with dignity and grace. I'd loved, and I'd served. My honor would remain intact until my last breath.

When I entered the villa, it was unusually dark inside. Maybe I can reach the Command Center. I thought. As I moved in that direction, I felt my body devoid of vitality. And behind my hollow eyes, my mind was idle. I no longer had the emotional strength nor the mental will to endure further reflection. I had come to final terms, my emotions shut down, my awareness visceral and focused on my surroundings.

After I made it to the Bar Room, I thought about Sue's warning. Where were they? Then I saw him sitting on the brown velvet sofa, just a few steps away from the command center table. Cyd was smiling at me in all his splendor. Surely my imagination was playing tricks on me. Even though I knew the answer I couldn't stop myself from asking.

"Is this a dream?"

"No. You're not dreaming. Nice suggested I visit you in your domain." Cyd said, with a look of amusement on his face.

"Why?" I asked, in a half whisper as I stared at him in disbelief.

"Because, Bob, there's nothing in our deal which includes you ending up dead." Then Cyd, elegantly attired in a well-tailored charcoal blue suit, white silk shirt, crimson tie and Italian loafers, sprung up from the sofa and spread out his arms as if to ask me what I thought.

"Spiffy outfit, no?" he grinned. "Pleasant allowed me to wear it, for the occasion of sparing your life."

"You mean to tell me you stopped the Cyprus Group attack on the villa?"

"Yes. Really a splendid way for me to begin the morning, don't you think? Those vengeful friends of yours I'm afraid left here in a rather undesirous state, and I don't think they have any intention of pursuing you further." I stood there speechless. Still convinced this was a dream, even as Cyd continued smiling, seeming intent on having me hear him out.

"Now, I'd say this is cause for celebration. How about a glass of wine?"

"So we're celebrating your interception of the Cyprus Group attack?"

"Well, sure, but our deal is what I'm most joyous about. Bob, you're still alive!

"Oh yeah, alive for what?!" I glared at him. The

agony of all I'd endured since this entire thing began bubbled to the surface, and I found it near impossible to contain my fury.

"Alive for what, Cyd?! What about the little detail about you and Pleasant double-crossing me and allowing my Fraternity members to die? What about sabotaging my plan and putting me through hell in the process?" Cyd sighed, then smiled again.

"Ah, details." Then he walked over to me and gently placed a hand on my right shoulder.

"Remember what I said to you Bob, you cannot possibly understand why we do what we do." His words enraged me and instinctively I shoved his hand off my shoulder.

"Don't give me that bullshit Cyd! Whatever the mystery behind what you do requires others to bear the suffering. Now tell me what you and Pleasant have done!"

"The best I can do is to say that we revere one who has proven his worth."

"Why are we even talking? Why have you done what you did? You told me I was on my own until I had all the Cyprus Group people on that scroll you gave me killed."

Cyd smiled, then he laughed a knowing laugh.

"I suggest you check the messages on your answering machine."

"What are you talking about? No calls came in and the teams we couldn't make contact no matter how many times we tried. They're probably all dead."

Despite my anger, curiosity got the better of me. I walked over to the machine and pushed the play button.

"Dave reporting. LA mission a success. Targets eliminated. No casualties." Dave's voice sounded confident and firm. I had him for dead. How was he still alive? I looked up, expecting to see Cyd's radiant smile, but he'd vanished.

Then I heard voices just outside the Bar Room, and the door opened. Frank, Dave and Kym walked in with confused expressions on their faces.

"Where in hell is everybody?" Frank asked. "This place looks like a damn ghost town, and you don't look so good."

"Right, well I had this feeling the Cyprus Group would attack the villa see and so I had Jacob Enterprises help me get everyone safely to Vancouver. I don't know what I was thinking." I casually shrugged my shoulders barely sure I could even buy the lie I was serving them.

"Jesus, Bob, the strain on you from everything that had gone wrong. It just finally caught up with you. No one always make the right decision. Go easy on yourself."

"Speaking of terrible decisions, when you arrived to Frank and Kym's aid did you encounter any difficulties?"

"Not once I arrived." Dave's eyes lit up.

"He was amazing!" Kym said, lacing her arm through Dave's as she looked up at him proudly. "He and Frank took over, and I stood out of the way." Then she rested her head against Dave's chest, love clear in her eyes, as she said to him, "Thanks again, hon, for being there."

"We got 'em, Bob, but we're sure glad to be back here." Frank said. Words escaped me, but I smiled for the first time in a long while. How was any of this possible? Pleasant and Cyd, whatever they did was incomprehensible. Cyd was right, I could never understand why and how they did what they did.

CHAPTER 25

THE NEXT ORDER OF BUSINESS was getting Jacob Enterprises on the line to request that they bring our people back to the Villa. Then I phoned Scott directly.

Kym was busy in the kitchen preparing coffee and snacks for us while Dave and Frank joined me in the command center to wait for calls to come in.

I was about to discover the extent of what Cyd and Pleasant were capable of. Not only did they ward off the Cyprus Group retaliation, but somehow had the power to reverse the events that had already taken place.

The phone started ringing incessantly.

"Mission completed in Las Vegas."

"San Francisco a success. Residents dead."

"Now, damn it, we're rolling!" Frank overjoyed at the reports coming in. Dave took the next call. After a few moments of intense discussion, he held up his mobile, shot me a gaze, and gasped, "I have Misha Knight on the phone. She's reporting success in Portland."

"Portland?! Impossible!" I vividly recalled my visit to Portland. The jet wasn't there. Then there was the party, the martini and being convinced we were finally shit out of luck.

I pushed a button on my mobile and joined in on Dave's conversation.

"Misha?"

"Yeah, Bob."

"You're reporting success in Portland?" I asked with obvious skepticism.

"Correct! Val and I took out our targets."

"And you encountered no difficulties?"

"None."

"Do you remember a party going on at the residence before you attacked?"

"No. No party. All was quiet. Why do you ask?" I paused. Then attempting to sound calm, my brows knit in confusion.

"It's just that some people have found that to be the case. You and Val okay?"

"Yeah, we're great! Got the timing just right."

"Okay and your jet? Was it waiting to bring you back?"

"We are aboard it now."

"Okay then, excellent work! See you soon." Then I nodded to Dave and did what I could to maintain my composure and mask my shock at how all was suddenly turning around. Calls continued to pour in.

"Philadelphia a success. All safe, on our way back."

"Cross Atlanta off the list. Mission achieved. Targets eliminated."

"Mission accomplished in St. Louis."

"Bingo on Corpus Christi." The Fraternity members of the Denver and Tucson missions also phoned in, reporting success.

Of all the calls that came in, the one that threatened my composure the most was Phoenix.

"Bob, Randy Erickson here. Phoenix mission was a success." At hearing Randy's words, my breath immediately caught in my throat. I couldn't stop myself from unloading on him.

"What in hell is the meaning of this bullshit joke, Randy? Damn it! Have you lost your mind? The resident targets weren't even home for Christ sakes! And Sue, the killer I brought to you, well she and I meticulously searched their place and couldn't find anyone on the property. And then you disappeared, so how in hell could you have killed anybody?"

There was a lengthy pause before Randy responded.

"Bob, surely you're the one joking. I never saw you or Sue. This flamboyant character gave me the name of Turbo, showed up, said he was the killer you sent. The targets were home. So yeah, we eliminated them."

I had the names of Vocarro's associates memorized. There was no one in the Cyd group by the name of Turbo. Oh, hell, I mused. Cyd's rectifying, well, he'd outdone himself on Phoenix.

"Look, Randy, I'm sorry. I'm just confusing your mission with another. Joke's on me, never mind. And excellent work!"

I could hear Randy's sigh of relief on the other end of the line. After he hung up, it took me a few moments to collect myself before announcing that the mission was a success.

I crossed Phoenix off the list and realized it was the last mission unaccounted for. The energy in the Command Center soared.

Frank, his eyes gleaming, walked over to me.

"We've done it, Bob! And what you've done is commendable beyond measure. The Fraternity owes you an immense debt of gratitude." Frank reached for my hand and shook it. Then Dave joined in and clapped me on the back.

"Keys to the City Bob, you damn well deserve them." I silently couldn't stop myself from wondering if I deserved such accolades. I was still trying to make sense of all that went wrong and all that Pleasant and Cyd magically made right. Then I thought about Sue. Was she still alive? Did Cyd have to kill her?

At that moment, Kym entered the Bar Room with coffee and an assortment of hors d'oeuvres.

"Kym it's over! All the teams reported in and they're on their way back." Kym hesitated before saying anything. Then as she let the news sink it, her expression turned to joy.

"No more killing?"

"No more killing," Dave said. She pulled Dave into a long embrace. And then he smiled and pulled away gently.

"It's Bob you should hug hon. He's the mastermind behind this whole operation." Before I could object and say that it wasn't necessary, Kym had me in a tight embrace.

"Thank you, Bob. Thank you! For your daring spirit. We couldn't have survived this without you."

"It's time for celebration. The hell with coffee, let's get some champagne!" Frank shouted. I watched as Dave, Frank, and Kym let loose. They'd each endured as much, if not more, emotional turmoil than I had. It was good to see them dance, toast each other, and smile. I joined in the celebration until exhaustion coupled with my preoccupation with Sue put an end to my capacity for a jovial mood. I needed to rest.

"Sorry, folks, I think my energy has given out. Carry on, but please excuse me."

"Get all the rest you need," Frank smiled. "You deserve it."

As soon as I entered my room, memories of Sue and what we shared flashed through my mind. I was beyond exhaustion; in grips of despair, digging my nails gently into my palms, I cried out Sue's name.

I knew Gloria's spirit would understand this yearning for another. Sue was just another once upon a time now. I couldn't resist sighing over what we'd lost forever. I wondered about Gloria's spirit and conceded to the realization that I'd never get to see it. No matter how much gratitude Frank and the others threw my way, I couldn't accept what happened as a win. Without Cyd and Pleasant's help, I would have failed miserably.

I needed sleep, but Sue's door caught my attention. I'd never crossed the threshold into her room. I got up and opened the door, unable to stop myself from entering. I flipped on the light and saw that the room was tidy, a wholesomeness about it. Then I noticed a folded sheet of paper, propped up against a pillow on Sue's bed. It looked like the one I'd seen the day she disappeared on the mission.

I ambled to the bed and gently unfolded it. As I suspected, the note was in Sue's elegant hand:

Bob, I love you! Forever. And forever, hold this love in your heart.

I felt a chill run through me, and I absentmindedly brought the unfolded sheet of paper to my chest, feeling the thumping of my heart reaching out and embracing Sue's message of love.

"Damn you, Pleasant." Then I felt it. I was becoming drowsy, dizzy for sleep. My body involuntarily slumped forward onto Sue's bed and I fell into an immediate and deep slumber.

At last I was in familiar territory. Though it was not where I wanted to be. Despite the beauty of the deep pooled desert oasis, and the masterful strokes that colored the world of my dreams, I could no longer succumb to the magic of it. I was, as Pleasant had proven, just a pawn in a game I couldn't understand. All I wanted was to see Gloria's spirit, but what I had to deliver came to fruition by magic and not my own deeds. What did Pleasant want with me now? To gloat?

Pleasant appeared then, again by the edge of the pool, cooking those strange meatballs of his, just like before. His weathered face and deep blue eyes lit up when he saw me.

"Bob, I was expecting you."

"Expecting me, why?"

"You do not seem happy to see me."

"You've got that right," I said, as I stared into his majestic eyes. "I've lost all trust in you. You've caused me great pain!"

"I see," He smiled, which always infuriated me. He and Cyd always calm while I was a raging ball of fury.

"Well, I will redress that, my friend."

"You're not my friend!"

"Someday, you'll see that even friendship can require one to embark on unexpected journeys, Bob. Now come sit down next to me. I have prepared the most delectable meal for us. Let us share in this together, and in fellowship discuss the matters that are most unsettling to you."

"Fellowship?" I sneered. "We have no fellowship Pleasant! That's all gone now!" Patting the ground beside him, Pleasant smiled once again.

"Even if you believe this to be true, we can still share a meal together."

"No! No! I'm on to your tricks. I'm eating none of those damn meatballs!" Pleasant snorted, then laughed, a powerfully infectious laugh.

"Well, you are right Bob. I have had to bring an end to my tricks, most of them. Nice has seen to that."

"Nice?"

"Have you forgotten? You mortals refer to Nice as

God. And in your vernacular, God has jumped all over my ass for misusing my tricks. Not a pretty sight, I can tell you. Now come sit down beside me and let us savor this luscious meal together."

"No tricks?" I asked skeptically.

"To be honest, perhaps only a small one. Enough to redress the pain you alluded to."

"Okay," I said reluctantly. I sat down beside him. Pleasant held up a plate with these strange-looking meatballs on it, and using his fingers, popped one into his mouth, and while chewing it, he pushed the plate toward me.

"Now you have one. Delicious taste for yourself." I used my fingers to pop a meatball into my mouth and chewed. Whatever was in these things, they were delicious, and I relished every bite. We ate in silence and with rising joy. By the time we emptied our plates, we were both delirious with laughter and joy. To remain seated upright, I had to get a firm grip on Pleasant's forearm lest I fall over from the incessant laughter that had overtaken me.

"This is the life! No need for questions, no need for answers. The pursuit for each is meaningless," Pleasant roared jovially, his words, like mine, beginning to slur. His laughter seemed to shake the ground beneath us. We enthusiastically gave each other hard thumps on our backs which caused us to lose our balance and wind up flat on our backs giggling like children. We laughed together until tears sprung from our eyes and our insides ached from the spasms that racked our bodies.

Then unexpectedly I became still, totally spent, lying on the ground I gazed up at the majesty of the sky. Pleasant had also become quiet and lay at my side also looking up into the sky.

"I needed the laughter. Needed to share it. It eased away the consequences of my actions." Pleasant said, his voice now quiet and contemplative.

I sat up then and looked down at Pleasant.

"When you say tricks, you mean the tricks you used to kill off the remaining Cyprus Group members the Fraternity couldn't touch?"

"Yes. I thought they were appropriate, given the circumstances, and Cyd agreed. But Nice thought otherwise, and he's proclaimed something else. It's about redressing you for your pain. Nice has proclaimed that you have fulfilled your part of our deal."

"What?! How? How can God, er Nice, feel I have kept my end of our deal? When I screwed everything up."

"Bob, you had the proper intent, and you carried out your mission in good faith. It was Cyd, and I who screwed things up."

"And you agree with Nice?"

"No one ever disagrees with Nice." I sat in silence for a moment, staring down at the grass.

"Wait, a minute. Let me see if I've got this straight. You're saying I've kept my end of our deal?"

"That's what I'm saying." A feeling of jubilance was starting.

"Then now you have to keep your end of the deal.

According to our agreement, I get to see and interact with Gloria's spirit."

"So, quit stalling! Where is it?!"

"But, Bob, I have already kept my end of our deal. You have already seen and interacted with Gloria's spirit."

"Oh, so you're lying to me now? You damn well know I haven't seen or interacted with Gloria's spirit, so how could you say that?"

"Ah, but you have," Pleasant beamed with a satisfying grin. "Sue Bishop."

"Sue?!"

"Yes. Gloria's spirit took the form of Sue Bishop. I thought your get-together in the outside world, in the flesh, would be a better arrangement than if it took place here. Give you a better go at it, shall we say?"

My body went numb before it transformed into anger.

"A better go at it? How could that be when I didn't know that Sue was Gloria's spirit?"

"Gloria's spirit could not tell you that." I wanted to strike him, punch him, get the rage out of me.

"How could you? If I had known that Sue was Gloria's spirit, our relationship would have unfolded much differently. It would have had more meaning, been more sacred and allowed me to share what was in my heart. To ask for forgiveness. And I wouldn't have thought she was a spy and lost valuable time with her."

I stopped to breathe and tried to regain control of my composure.

"You robbed me of that. How could you be so cruel? First you use me like a pawn in the war against the Cyprus Group, and then you taunt me with the thing I most wanted."

"You were engaged in the business of cruelty, Bob. Your circumstances of battle with the Cyprus Group left no other course in your relationship with Sue than what it was without creating greater problems. We did the best we could. It was a delicate matter protecting Sue and fitting her into the scheme of things while preventing her from harm and allowing her some freedom to take action to protect you. You can thank Gloria's spirit for that."

Finally, I said, "Whatever. But you tricked me again, you bastard! You have any more of those meatballs? I think we were better off laughing!"

"Now don't start feeling sorry for yourself, Bob."

"How could I not Pleasant?! You misled me, and now I can see I'll never interact with Gloria's spirit on my terms."

"That's not exactly true, Bob."

"What? Can you have her spirit appear now?"

"Something better."

"I'm listening."

"Nice feels the same way you do in not knowing that Sue was Gloria's spirit when you were with her. To make amends, and redress your pain, Nice has ordered me to give you and Sue, Gloria's spirit, one month together in the outside world to engage in whatever you wish. And Sue will be free to tell you she is Gloria's spirit."

"You would do that?!"

"What Nice orders me to do, I do without question. But mind you, when the month is up, Gloria's spirit must return here, and Sue Bishop will no longer exist. Is that acceptable? Is that worth sharing laughs over?"

I nodded and overwhelmed with emotion I threw my arms around Pleasant.

"Thank you! And Thank Nice!"

"Oh, Nice knows you'll be grateful. Sue is waiting. Goodbye, Bob."

The dream ended. When I awoke, I was still in Sue's bed and I could hear the sound of soothing music and then I felt the soft contours of Sue's body lying beside me. She turned and looked at me with a tender look in her eyes.

"What took you so long, darling?

ABOUT THE AUTHOR

GERALD G. GRIFFIN was born in Flint, Michigan. He is a graduate of Michigan State University where he received his MA and PhD in psychology. Since his days in private practice he has penned more than five mystery & suspense novels. His most recent titles include, 'The Gods of Winter' and 'Gods, Dreams & Love' both from his Bob Daniel's romantic suspense series. He is now retired and continues to write full-time from his home in Gainesville, Georgia.

Thank You for Reading

Gods, Dreams & Love Book 2 in the Bob Daniels Romantic Suspense Series

If you enjoyed the book, please consider leaving a short review on Amazon or your website of choice.

Reviews help both readers and writers.
They are an easy way to support good work and help to encourage the continued release of quality content.

Connect with Gerald G. Griffin
www.authorgeraldgriffin.com

Want the latest from the Brooklyn Writers Press?

Browse our complete catalog.
www.brooklynwriterspress.com